In Her Skin:

Growing Up Trans

a young adult novel

Trina Sotira

𝓜𝓊𝓈𝓮Write
PRESS

First published as an ebook in the United States of America
by MuseWrite Press 2012

ISBN 978-0-9899609-0-8 (ebook)
ISBN 978-0-9899609-2-2 (pbk.)

PUBLISHER'S NOTE

This is a work of fiction. Names, characters, places, and incidents
are a product of the author's imagination based on a true account
dictated by a transgender male.

First Printing 2016
Copy Editor: Crystal Fencke
Cover design: Robin Ludwig Designs
Formatting: Polgarus Studio

For Chas

"I'm with everyone and yet not
Just wanna be myself.

Hey you said that you would love to try
some
Hey you said that you would love to die
some
In the middle of a world on a fishhook
you're the wave
you're the wave
you're the wave…

I miss the one that I love a lot."

-Bush, "Swallowed"

1.

There's no way I can go in the girls' bathroom packed with makeup abusing suburbanites, geeked up from a Chicago tourist high. I don't even look like a girl anymore. Heidi gives me this sympathetic face like she's totally feeling what I'm feeling. I want to hug her because she's always the only one that understands me.

"Go on. I'll meet ya by the Bean," she says, and walks into the girls' bathroom. I'm left by myself, looking at that weird outline of a guy on the sign that tells me this is where I should be. But it doesn't even look like a guy. The only thing that looks different is that it's someone in pants. And the girls' sign has someone in a dress, which is weird because a lot of girls don't always wear dresses.

I've got little time to get all philosophical on the toilet signs, so I bail into the guys' room. The smell of pee and powder-scented sanitizer is overwhelming, cooked by a hyperactive heating system. All the stall doors are closed. Two men stand against the urinal wall with their pants open.

As I'm waiting for a stall, I hear laughter behind me.

1

"Yo. Troy? Is that you dude?" I turn around. It's C and the guys from the skate park. That one rabid-looking A-hole is there too. Suck.

The A-hole says, "Dude, what are you waiting for? There are six open urinals, and you're waiting for a stall?"

A heavy old guy opens a stall door, tucking a folded newspaper under his arm. He disappears behind a wall of sinks.

C leans close. "Ugh. Sick. You're not gonna go in there, are you? It's gonna smell like that guy's ass vomit!"

I laugh. "Shut up!"

The guys head for the urinal and unzip almost simultaneously like they're part of some Broadway show. I look away. Don't wanna see what they've got down there. They stare at me—wondering why I'm not at the urinal with them.

I'm about to have an accident and choose to swallow every ounce of whatever pride I had. "I've gotta drop a goose," I say, holding my stomach.

C and the other guy laugh hard so some of their pee loses aim and flings at the wall.

I push the silver bracket closed on the stall door and try to catch my breath. Thank God I escaped a public pants drop. For special effects, I blow some air into my arm so it sounds like an overeater at an all-you-can-eat buffet. But I wonder if anyone can even hear me with the other sounds of running water, flushing toilets, and air dryers.

What's weird is that I don't want to leave the stall. It's hard to think about walking past the other guys at the urinals. But the smell of warm elephant dung becomes too much to bear, and I gag. I've gotta get out of here.

I wanna be all cute and fun by the time I get back to Heidi, but something isn't sitting right after the bathroom thing. Like I wonder if people are looking at me and can tell that I'm really still a girl.

I find Heidi close to the Bean sculpture, standing next to a thirty-foot tall guy on stilts. He blends in with the clouds and the Chicago skyline, while he twists and turns a balloon.

When Heidi sees me, she holds out a sword-shaped balloon. "For you." She hands it to me. "I'm getting a flower."

Her smile starts to deflate. "Tirzah—" She stops. "I mean, Troy. Are you alright? You look kinda pale or something." I swallow at the part about her calling me Tirzah. It's gonna take a long time until I'm one-hundred percent Troy.

"Just fine, Hafsa," I say, trying to mimic Heidi's father's thick Bengali accent.

The stilt-guy hands Heidi her flower. She flicks her wrist as the balloon bends from the force of her arm.

"Thank you, my prince of tallness," she says with her head looking up at the man. He slouches down to shake her hand, his knees shaking the material of his orange clown pants. I worry he'll fall.

"Maybe it's time for Beanage. I know if I'm ever down about anything it always makes me feel better when I stare at huge silver things."

"Yeah. Silver things equal major happiness. Totally

3

agree," I say, hesitating before taking her hand.

We head up a small flight of stairs. Kids and adults, moms and old people are crowded under the center of the Bean. It's massive and silver, an arching mirror above my head. We stand near the sculpture and our heads look like elongated alien people—the longer pieces of my hair appear to pull my face toward freakish distortion.

We get inside the structure. "Huh-ha!" Heidi laughs. "Whoop, whoop!" she yells. The sounds echoes back.

Then I get this weird caffeinated idea and say, "Faaaaaaart," in a super deep voice so it almost sounds like an actual fart—one from someone sitting on a vinyl booth at Denny's.

People are looking around at each other, wondering if we're playing the smelt-it-dealt-it game. Wondering who said it.

Heidi is cracking up and staring up at the Bean's center, her teeth looking super white like on a commercial for toothpaste.

"Faaaaaaaaaahhhhhhrrrrrrrt," she bellows with the lungs of an opera singer. It's like the most beautiful wind chime ringing through the roundness of the Bean. Now everyone stares at us. Some younger kids are laughing at us. More like laughing with us.

"Come over here," Heidi says, pulling me towards the side of the Bean that touches the ground. She squeezes herself between the cement sidewalk and part of the sculpture so her head is looking up at the underside of the Bean. I do the same.

We're lying—just the two of us—underneath our distorted reflection. Heidi still looks beautiful with her dark hair spread in a fan shape around her head like wings. But I look weird. Lost. Confused. I still have girls' eyes and a girl's mouth. If I were in a dress, I'd look butchy.

I know that this is the worst place to cry because one, it's the middle of the day, and two, we're in the middle of freakin' Chicago, and three, it's one of the biggest tourist attractions, and four, I'm not supposed to let Heidi see me like this.

"Oh my god, T, are you alright?" Heidi asks, looking up at the image of us.

I can see redness in my face, but can't find my tears in my reflection.

I swallow on some phlegmy stuff in my throat and wipe my eyes with the back of my wrist. "I'm alright. Just. This just sucks. I mean, it's all cool here, but when we get back home we'll never have this moment again. I can't pull off the guy thing at school or in front of your parents. I'm getting sick of being able to be myself only in the city."

"That's what's so awesome about the city, though. No one knows us here." She stops. "And Baba, well, he's got so much on his mind anyway." Heidi puts her hands above her head and picks at her fingers.

"Like what?" I ask.

"No. Nothing. He still keeps talking about moving, but who knows."

And then I get this sick feeling like the people in the Bean are just as distorted-looking as my life. "You're my happiness. You can't leave me," I say, sounding stupidly desperate.

Heidi turns her head and I face her so our faces are resting on the cold cement. "It's not up to me," she says.

"But maybe it is," I answer, watching the bubbled reflection of us. The only way I'm gonna get through the rest of this day in a good mood is if I convince myself that Heidi won't ever leave me. But I read somewhere that we always return to the place where we started. Like how we're born needing diapers and we die needing diapers. How we all wanna leave our homes to go out and find ourselves, but we always wanna go back home once we get to wherever it is that we were going. I know she'll go back home soon. But somehow when I look at Heidi in our little corner of the Bean, it's like the first day we met. She's still Happy Heidi and I'm still Tomboy Tirzah. Even though I can see all these tourists around us, feeling the smooth silver sides of the sculpture and looking at themselves in the round reflection, it's still like we're the only ones.

Some girl with super-long hair crouches down so she's practically sitting with us. "Hey! Do you mind if I take a picture of you guys? How you were just now—lying next to each other?"

Heidi smiles big. "Sure. Of course." She looks at me. Her eyes widen. I follow Heidi's glance to the stranger's press badge: *Chicago Tribune*.

We find our spot back under the Bean and look up at our reflection.

The photographer twists and turns the round part of her

camera, clicking and flashing. "Perfect. Absolutely perfect," she says.

We're both blushing. "What's this for?" I ask.

"Oh, I'm doing a story on fun things young couples can do in the city. And you guys look perfect for the cover shot."

"How cool is that!" I say. She thinks we're a couple.

Heidi elbows my side and we get the giggles. The lady snaps away.

When she's finished, the reporter pulls out a small notepad. "Can I get your names?"

We squirm our way out from under the Bean so we're sitting up.

"I'm Heidi," she says, "and this is my friend, Tirzah."

Friend? Tirzah not Troy. Heidi knows that when we're in the city I get to be a guy.

"WTF?" I whisper in Heidi's ear.

She smiles. "It's the Tribune, T. Everyone's gonna see us."

All the empty holes in my heart split open again.

2.

Rain-drenched bangs cover my eyes, and I whip my head to see the soccer ball flying at my face. Springing in mid-air, I thrust my body forward to stop it. A thud echoes into my heart as the ball bounces off my chest, landing on the out-of-bounds line.

My father yells, "Nice save, Tirzah!" I pretend not to hear him and put my head back into the last two minutes of the game.

My breasts hurt like hell, but I block out the pain. I try to pretend like that part of my body really isn't mine.

After the game, I'm rubbing my legs on the sideline when Dad comes up to me. He stares at the pink octagon prints that have formed on my thighs from the soccer ball's attempts to charge into my goal.

Dad slaps my back, and his Illinois University rain poncho makes my bare arm feel even colder.

"You were fantastic!" He looks toward the stands, probably to see if Mom ever showed. The bleachers are bare.

He continues, "Two more weeks until Coach Shoals will

be at Regionals, watchin' you one last time. Just gotta fight a little harder. You've got this. You know, I saw those low saves, but I think you could throw your body into them more. We'll work on it."

I see the empty stands, like they've been used and left for dead. If I go to Illinois University and play on the girls' team, I'll die. I wonder how much a tombstone costs anyway, and can I buy one at the college bookstore?

"Tirzah—" Dad nudges my side.

I can't think about improving anything right now when I'm this tired, so I muster, "Yeah. I'll try and fix my game." But there's a rush of energy when I see Heidi walking out of the locker room doors, making her way toward us.

Dad squeezes my hand. "You were the star, Tirzah. God, you make it look so easy."

I'll say anything right now to get him to go away for a minute. "Thanks! And you're still the loudest fan. For sure, Dad!"

He gives me that look like I've made him so proud. "Alright. I'm gonna head home." I tell him I'll see him in a while. He walks down the track toward the parking lot.

And then Heidi's by my side, lighting me up. "Great game, Tirzah." She bumps my hip.

I look around the field, but everyone's gone by now. It's just me and Heidi.

"Thanks. Four goals—you're not so bad either," I say. We slap fives.

"Pick me up for practice? Before seven a-m?" Heidi puts her hands together and rests her face on them, pretending to fall asleep. "No sleeping in this time, you hear?"

I'm dreading another early wake-up. "But if I'm there on time, anyone who's late has to lick my cleats."

"Deal," she says, all flirty-like, and touches her first finger to the tip of my nose. I push it away, but still hold on to her hand.

The next morning, it's five minutes to seven when I pull into Heidi's driveway. She's on the front porch of her townhouse with her head covered by her hoodie. The sun brushes her face and lights up her cinnamon-colored skin. She walks toward my car. Her father stands guard in his pajama bottoms and tank top, covering the span of their small bay window. I wave. He rises up on his tip-toes and stares intently, as if checking to see if any guys are in the car.

"Bye!" Heidi calls out.

Mr. Chaudhary waves back and stays in the window, still watching as I pull out.

We're turning the corner, leaving her subdivision, when Heidi says, "Nice bags under your eyes. What time were you up 'til?"

She digs through her black leather purse.

"Oh, I don't know, midnight." I turn my head to keep focused on the road as she holds out a tube of makeup.

"What do you want me to do with this?"

"Cover up."

I press the gas and turn up the radio. "Yeah, right! These bags make me look all tough and shit, don't they?"

"Uh. No. They make you look cracked out." She puts the makeup tube back in her purse.

"Whatev. Maybe I wanna look badass." I sink lower into my seat and gangsta-lean to the right.

She smirks in a way that makes me think she might actually want to be more than just friends.

Some love song comes on the radio and Heidi grabs for the volume button. I would rather wear a bra than listen to a girl complain about hetero-heartbreak. But I sing just to hear our duet.

When we get to practice, Coach Rip is already outside the field house, waiting for us. "There she is, late, late, late." Rip taps his stop watch. "They aren't going to take that at I-U, Maxon." I don't think he's called me Tirzah in four years.

"Oh, what is it 7:05? Come on, gimme a break."

Rip holds out a DVD that looks like someone burned him a copy. "I've got some videos for you to watch. Meet me in the gym office in two minutes."

Heidi whispers in my ear, "Ooh, I'd like to meet him in the office." Then she gets all runway—swishing her hips as she walks toward the fieldhouse doors.

"Easy, trashy!" I shout as she heads outside to find our team on the soccer field.

In Rip's office, I stare at a small TV and try to analyze the pro-goalies' techniques. The jumps, the dives, the saves and throws.

Rip pauses the DVD, "What do you see there?"

"They're pretty good—die hard goalies." I'm not sure what he's getting at.

"No, Maxon, they aren't that good. You're better. You're one of the best. But you need to keep your head in the game.

That's what's gonna get you on top at Illinois University. You've gotta keep focused. Here. Watch this." He skips ahead to a part where the goalie is diving at the ball. My phone rings.

"You shouldn't have that thing on you right now. This is practice."

My brother, HP, is calling. Really Hank Peter, but I call him Hair Pie because of this massive fluff of chest hair that creeps out of his v-necks.

"I've gotta take this. He never calls unless it's some crisis."

Rip pauses the tape and rolls his eyes, while I bring my phone in the hall.

"What?" I whisper.

"Where're my keys, ass munch?" HP sounds out of breath.

"How would I know?"

"You're the only one who has my other set."

"Not true—did ya check the key hanger in the kitchen?"

"That's why I'm calling you."

Rip sticks his face out the door. "Let's go, Maxon."

"I gotta hang up," I say into the phone. "Practice, remember? I'm sure your keys are somewhere, dude. Lemme call you later."

HP responds, "Oh, and mom called. Something about meeting her at, uh, something-something. I don't know."

"Where?" I ask.

"No clue," he says, chomping chips into the phone.

"God, you're such a douchebag!" I snap.

"Love you, too, Tit-zah," he answers. I cringe.

I close my cell and leap back into Rip's office, trying to avoid eye contact. Sure he's wearing the look of death.

"You know, Maxon, if you want that scholarship you'd better get your priorities straight." And that's when he loses me. The priorities lecture. Adults who think teens have no priorities bother me. Big time.

"I know. I gotta get a free ride. Otherwise I'll be at a community college, playing on a co-ed indoor league with guys with beer bellies. I get it." But playing with guys doesn't sound so bad.

"Finally!" Rip slaps me five. "We've only got a couple weeks until Regionals." He passes me the soccer ball—hard. I trap it with the bottom of my foot. "Remind me again, Rip. I got it, two weeks. Thanks, padre!" Deep inside I'm thinking about the dorm showers at Regionals. How am I gonna hide my body?

3.

We're by the girls' fitting room at Target when Heidi hands me her purse, a box of Cocoa Puffs, and two pairs of jeans.

"Wait one sec," she says, sifting through a clothing rack. "I needs me some lovin'."

Heidi pulls out a turquoise sundress and looks at the price tag. "Twelve dollars. Seriously? I've gotta try this on." She hands me the dress, so now I'm holding all of her stuff, while she keeps looking through the clearance racks.

A minute later, she takes the clothes from me, slips into a fitting room, and leaves me alone with her purse and some Cocoa Puffs. I'm so hungry I could just rip open the box.

Target is packed with at-home moms and their grabbing children. A shopping cart of trouble is only three feet from me and this boy, probably five, is staring. I'm used to it.

"Mom, why's he standing there?" The boy is trying to smile at me but years of stranger-danger etiquette have left their mark.

The mom leans on the shopping cart's handle. "Sheeee is probably waiting for someone, honey. There's a fitting room right there." I smile at her, and nod my head at the boy. He's just made my week, and has no idea. If only my parents and everyone else could see that I was really supposed to be a guy, then life would be golden.

Heidi opens the dressing room door, her bare feet tip-toeing on the linoleum floor.

"This is the perfect dress," she says. It is. Her eyes gleam, and every part of me is smiling.

"Hmm," she says. "Think I should get it? I mean, do you think my dad will lemme wear it?"

"I don't know, he might not, but still you look gorgeous. Yeah. Get it."

"K." She twirls on her toes.

Checking behind us, the mother and her psychic son have left. We're alone. Heidi tip-toes to the dressing room, looking back at me, as if she's pulling me in with her eyes.

The fitting room door closes. I am left alone. Through a crack I watch her pull off the dress, slide her arms, one at a time, out of the straps. Her breasts show through the thinness of her bra. I press myself against the outside of the dressing room door: my hand flat and opened on the smooth, white surface. My cheek smashed into its coldness. I close my eyes and picture myself in there with her. Helping her pull the dress over her head in the small space of fluorescent light and mirrors. I picture myself kissing her head and ears, her neck, down.

But then the static from a walkie-talkie gets louder as footsteps get closer to the fitting room. A long-haired lady asks, "Is someone in there?"

I giggle, wondering if she knows what I was just thinking.

"Yep, I'm just about done," Heidi calls out from inside.

"Alright, just checkin'," the clerk says, and continues on to the next room, capturing loose clothing and bulking them together in her arms.

In Heidi's kitchen, her mother is cooking chicken in oil on the stove. There's a cloud of smoke around her that the stove fan has struggled to capture. My stomach growls from the scents of curry and coconut, and I hope I'm invited for dinner just so I can spend more time with Heidi.

"Hafsa, what did you buy?" Heidi's mom steps away from the stove, tugging at the bag.

"Just a dress," Heidi says. Her mother pulls the dress from the bag, holds it up, and presses the seam against her daughter's thighs.

"Pretty short, don't you think?"

"No, it's fine Mom. Come on." Heidi waves her hands to shoo her mom away.

"Not for school, though, Hafsa. Your father won't let you out of the house in

this." Mrs. Chaudhary looks at me and raises her eyebrows, waiting for me to agree.

I raise my eyebrows back at her and press my lips together to let her know I'm not sure what to say. Actually, I'm weirded out by their conversation, wondering if I should walk into the family room, or stand there and watch Heidi in another battle for independence. It's true, her father wouldn't let her wear that to school, but I wish her mom would be cool and let Heidi celebrate this small moment.

"Whatever, then, I'll just wear it here. Better, Mom?" Heidi picks a piece of spiced chicken from the pan on the stove and eats it.

"Mmm," she says looking my way. "Want some?"

I shake my head and Heidi pushes a piece in my mouth. I smirk and chew as the front door opens. Heidi's father walks in, his stomach pushing through his leather coat.

He slips his shoes off. "Bi-smi Allah ar-rahman ar-rahim." He says that all the time. Heidi told me once that it's like praising God.

"My feet! Another day with the general public takes its toll on my body. When are those people ever going to learn to read a museum map instead of having me walk them everywhere?" Mr. Chaudary bends over rubbing his right foot, as I imagine the smell transferring from his sweaty sock to his palm.

I can't remember when her dad didn't complain about the tourists at the Field museum. Each time he does, it becomes so obvious how much he misses his job in Dhaka where he was a professor. Sometimes I wonder why they stay in Chicago, why he batters his body as a docent, and another part-time job at a factory just to live here. But then I remember the stories they've told about how poor people are in Bangladesh. I totally get why he puts up with it.

"Hello, Tirzah," he shakes my hand. "How's our favorite Blakean girl?" Mr. Chaudhary loves my name, and the fact that my parents named me after a poem written by William Blake called "To Tirzah."

"Just divine, sir," I say with a British accent.

He kisses Heidi's forehead, then walks over to his wife and kisses her neck. I think of my dad without mom—alone since the divorce. I should be at home.

"You know, I'd better go. My dad's probably waiting for me for dinner."

"Oh, alright, I'll see you tomorrow, OK?" Heidi hugs me. Her hair has taken on all of the yummy smells from the kitchen. I say my goodbyes to her parents and find my way out.

On my drive home, I'm picturing her body in the dressing room. I want to turn my car around and go back to her house. Maybe we could go study in her room. Maybe something would finally happen between us.

After dinner, I'm in the bathtub at home, hiding my body underneath a layer of lavender bubbles. My breasts peek over the tops of the bubbles, and I pull more pillows of white toward my body, covering my chest. Dad's razor rests on the side of the tub, and I think about putting it on my skin, slicing across my left breast, cutting it off like some eighteenth-century writer Dad told me about, and her mastectomy without anesthesia. She was conscious during the entire procedure. And she lived.

If I cut my breasts off in the tub, the blood would run all over, but I'd still survive. I could put towels on top of me and use gauze bandages to heal myself. And if it got really bad, I'd have to go to the hospital, and they'd have to fix the problem—give me flat skin across my chest. I could finally have the chest that should have been mine to begin with.

With the razor in hand, I pull my left breast to the center of my body, so it's flat, and start to cut at my skin. The hot water seeps into the incision. It burns. I can't go through with it—What if I bleed to death? What if I die in the bathtub? Heidi. What about Heidi?

Sanity slips back into my head, and I force myself to get out of the tub. If it wasn't for Heidi, I'd be dead already. She's the only thing worth living for.

———◆———

Heidi gets off of work at four, and I pick her up in front of Partytime. She's holding two balloons, one a deep blue and one pale silver.

She ducks into my car. "I got you something," she says, and hands me the blue balloon. The words "Over the Hill" are written in white.

"Ok. So it's like that, huh?" I tease. Last week she gave me a dozen "Grand Opening" balloons, and we hung them from my car's antennae. We drove real slowly while the balloons bopped around in the air. People on Main Street stared. We laughed hysterically the entire time after one old guy asked us where our grand opening was. I slouched down a little in my seat and tried to act all gangsta. "It's right here." I moved my hand like I was shaking a pair of dice. "This *is* the grand opening, yo." While the guy frowned at us and turned away. "Crazy kids."

In my passenger seat, Heidi pushes her nose into her balloon and looks my way, making an imprint of her face in the silver latex. "Crazy kids," she mocks, opening and closing her mouth like she's gumming the balloon with the toothless mouth of an elderly person. She pulls her face out of the balloon, revealing the word "Surprise!" on its exterior.

"I see," I say, "so it's like an 'Over the Hill' surprise party. Like surprise, you're over the hill!" I back out of my parking spot. "Ha ha! That's such a terrible thing to do to someone. Surprise, you're an old mutha!"

Heidi laughs and her tongue touches her bottom teeth. "Or it could be a somewhere over the hill lies a surprise party! Like once you climb over the hill, you'll get a surprise!"

"Totally. I like that party better," I say. And then I get an idea.

Five minutes later, I'm parking in the Fair Oaks Lake lot. It's pretty empty except for two cars parked at opposite ends.

"What's here?" Heidi asks, as if we've never been.

"You'll see. Grab your balloon." She does, and we start off on the path, climbing up a steep hill. The grass is still brown from the winter, and I wish it were a little softer for what I want to do. But it'll have to work.

We're up high, looking down at the forest; tall trees with newborn leaves spread for over a mile. It's vast and gorgeous, like my English teacher Mr. Kipp's pictures of Hampstead Heath—where British poets used to write.

I find a patch of grass that seems untouched and lie down.

"My, my, I've nevah been so high in the sky befowah," Heidi says, pretending to be Southern or something.

Rough grass pokes my head as I laugh. "Oh, baby, I could

take you places you nevah been. To places that make you nevah wanna return to the place you came from." And then she is lying next to me. Shoulder to shoulder.

I put my arm in the air, my balloon extending on its string heading straight for the puffy clouds. The phrase "Over the Hill" bops around above us.

Heidi puts her arm up, too. Her balloon sparkles in the sky.

"See," I say, "It's a surprise over the hill party!" Heidi leans toward me.

"But what's the surprise?"

"Hmmm." I pretend to think. Then I roll to my side and put my head on her stomach.

"Mmmm." She says. "What kinda shurprize party is thish anywaysh? I'm over the hill, see, and I thought we were gonna celebrate or something." I look up at her face. She folds her lips in so her mouth looks toothless again. "You youngstersh are shooo tricky."

She laughs and my head shakes from her stomach's movement. I hear water jiggle like the quickness of her heart.

I roll away from her nervousness and lie flat on the ground.

"Balloon race?" I ask.

"Totally! I'll accept that challenge." She's back to Heidi. No longer Southern or elderly. Just my Heidi.

"Ready, set, GO!" I say, and release the string.

We watch as our balloons float higher and higher away from us. My blue one keeps its lead over Heidi's silver balloon. We squint while they become smaller and smaller specks of faded color until they disappear among the clouds.

4.

It's the first warm day of spring when people seem to come out of their houses like ants piling out of a mound of sand. I'm on my board skating down the sidewalk when Ty catches up to me.

"Yo," he says, "did ya do your American Studies?" His left leg gives two strong pushes on the sidewalk, and he passes me.

I skate down a driveway and into the street. "Sure I did. It was easy, why?" I'm now ahead of him and he takes the second driveway into the street so we're side by side.

"No, dude, I didn't get it done. It's crazy—all that research and shit." His face is red around his mouth, and his pimples look like they're flaring up in the cool breeze.

"Smoking a j-bird again, huh, dumbass?" I put my fingers to my lips and pretend to inhale until I'm choking.

"Shut up! It was a freakin' Scooby Doo marathon. JC and I couldn't stop laughing. He was popping wood over Velma's skirt and all, and I don't know, we just couldn't stop."

"Whatever. Sure, you can copy my paper, but if you get caught I'm saying you held me at pocket-knife point with a group of stormtroopers and made me give it to you." We hit school property and simultaneously stomp on our boards. They fly up and we catch them like some freaky rehearsed stunt.

I pull the worksheet out of my bag, cringing at the hour and a half I spent on it, and pass it over to Ty. I wish I didn't always give into him, but I'd do anything to keep on his good side.

"Right on, Maxon," he says, and heads into a crowd of people.

I follow behind but lose him to a group of football players. I never feel safe around tall muscular guys, afraid that one day they'll slam me into a wall and out me for being a manly chick. It happened, you know—to a guy—and he barely made it. Spent a month in the hospital with broken bones just because a rumor spread that he was dating another guy. The football players couldn't handle gay blood in the locker room so they all pounded him until he couldn't walk again.

I want to walk. I need my legs just in case I decide to run away some day.

In first hour gym, we're in the second week of our bowling unit, sliding balls down the four lane alley of our high school basement. Rip's leg pulls behind him like some Grecian Olympian and I'm jealous of his ass muscles. I want a tight muscular ass instead of my flat pancake butt, which hides nicely in carpenter's jeans with a gazillion pockets.

"Maxon, glad you could make it," Rip calls out as his ball crashes into the triangle of pins at the end of the lane.

"Kingpin, baby!" He shouts while people clap. I find a seat next to Michelle and Skye and their clique.

Skye is looking at my button-down short-sleeve shirt. I've got a t-shirt underneath and my tight sports bra beneath that. I look down to make sure my chest is hidden. All good.

"Wanna be partners?" Skye asks, always trying to get closer to me since we messed around.

"OK, but today, whoever has the lowest score is gonna have to lick the thumb hole."

"Shut up, sick-ass!" Skye shouts. Yesterday the loser had to slide into the pins on their belly. Luckily, it was Sludge, our resident garbage disposal. Rip had a conniption, threatening us to shut down the alley if we didn't quit.

Skye stands up and pulls her shirt down to cover a one-inch section of skin that's showing between her shirt and jeans. I wish she hadn't done that.

She pounds her feet after rolling the ball into the gutter, while Sludge yells, "Ball licker!"

"Shut up, Sludge, or I'm gonna push your head into the ball wash."

"Oh yeah, I'd like to see that." Sludge puts his hand in front of his crotch and pretends to rub someone's head. "Wash 'em, bitches!" He shouts, and I'm laughing. I know he's not talking to me.

"God you're so sick!" Skye smacks Sludge's thick back, and he makes a face like he enjoys the abuse. "You're up, Tirzah."

I slip my fingers down into the bowling ball holes and line up my stance, just like Rip showed us. Staring down the lane toward the pins, I toss the ball gently and watch it roll right toward the triangle of targets. CRASH!

"You're such a douche, always trying to make me look bad." Sludge knocks my arm, and puts his hand up to slap five. I give a deep-throated HUH! and nudge him back.

"Tirz, did ya hear about Chris Jones's car?" Michelle asks as she picks a ball from the rack. I shake my head no.

"Yeah, someone threw a brick through his window out by Flanders." Our high school sits next to a demolished thorium plant once called Flanders. I swear it's the reason we're all so fucked up. Thorium probably leaked into the ground and into the water pipes—creeping up through the water fountains and into our bloodstreams.

"A brick? No shit. Do they know who did it?"

Michelle lines up to toss the ball. "No, but I totally think it was Ty and those guys."

"Dude, shut up. Ty wouldn't ruin someone's car like that." I'm always defending him.

"That kid gets so jacked up on steroids and weed—I wouldn't put it past him."

I take my seat back by Skye, sliding on the round plastic base. There's no way Ty would ever ruin someone's car. Even if it was Chris Jones's—the biggest prick at Trinity.

Three class periods later and I'm at my locker when Heidi finds me for lunch. "You'll never guess who asked me out this weekend."

"Asked you out? OK. Who?"

"JC! Freakin' JC! You know how we've been working on that gravity project together. Well, we had the presentation today, and it went totally well, like, we just flowed talking together." Her cheeks are all red and I want to remind her to breathe. "So we sit back down at our lab tables, and he scribbles in his notebook 'wanna hang out on Friday?' only he doesn't spell Friday out, he abbreviates it, and isn't that so cute?"

My back is against the locker, hoping it'll keep me steady so I don't sway back and forth or shake from feeling sick. "What about *baba*?"

"Dude, that's where you come in. I could never tell my dad. You know that. I'm just gonna say that I'm going out with you, and maybe you could even come to my house and pick me up or something, and then I'll have JC get me from your house."

I force a smile and try to keep my eyes wide so I match some of Heidi's enthusiasm when really all I want to do is grab her and ask her, What the fuck, JC, isn't he the biggest dildo here? But I can't ruin her happy moment. And JC has one thing going for him—his one-inch plastic toy monkey named Funky Fresh that is cute as hell. I even kissed it once for good luck.

"Sure. No big deal. Just let me know what time and I'll come get you." I cave.

Heidi hugs me, tight, and I can feel her chest on my chest, her lips by my neck. This is torture.

In English class, Mr. Kipp reads John Keats and although I can barely understand the poem "Bright Star," he tells us that the poet wrote it for his love, Fanny Brawne. Then he shares a letter where Keats tells Fanny, "I almost wish we were butterflies and liv'd but three summer days—three such days with you I could fill with more delight than fifty common years could ever contain." I close my eyes for just a second and think about the beauty of those words.

If Heidi and I were butterflies I would live three days with her and die just so we could be together, flying around the world. If only for three days the world would know how much I loved her, and she would know. I would no longer have to hide behind this skin.

Mr. Kipp reads, but I am lost imagining a world where people weren't divided into groups of boys and girls, men and women. I'm drawing a butterfly in black on my forearm and the pen goes deep. It hurts, but the pain feels good. Maybe I can scrape away a layer of my skin so everyone can see who I am on the inside. But who am I? A girl who likes girls? There's way more to it.

———◆———

When school gets out I take the train to the Oak Park stop and meet mom at Buzz Café. She's texted directions and shared a link with the menu. As if.

Buzz is packed with Friday night hipsters. A strange choice coming from mom who usually picks restaurants that require a translation dictionary. Mom waves frantically from the café window. Making a scene, for sure. As I approach, her tiny squeal turns shrill when she gets a peek at my outfit: some grungy vintage jeans and a men's button-down.

"Huuuuuh!" She gasps. "Tirzah, what is THIS?" Her boney hand traces the outline of my side. She tugs at my necktie; disgusted.

And I thought I looked pretty fly.

"Goodwill, Mom. Love it?" I wait. She frowns. "OK. No. Well, look around," I say, "This is the new hip." I wave my hands in front of me like I'm on display—the prize in some cheesy gameshow.

"You don't even WEAR glasses." She squeaks and pokes at my black frames.

Squeezing her sides in a massive hug, I attempt to drop the whole Q and A thing.

The hostess flags us over to find a seat. We weave in and out of wood tables, through different conversations like a roadmap into the mind of a twenty-something hipster: "Can you believe it?" "And then she said no. Like freaking no, I won't marry you." "I've never felt this strongly about anything in my entire life." "Yeah, you should hit that thing with your stick."

Our table is underneath a dotted Ray Bradbury face with the numbers 451 splattered in red paint across the canvas. It's bad as hell and I wanna buy it with my nonexistent funds. The life of a thousandaire is tough, man.

Mom orders an iced tea from the waiter and I say water with lemon. We sit for a while, looking around, while I try to listen to the rest of the conversation from the table of guys behind us. The ones who were talking about hitting something with their sticks.

They're saying something else now, like, "But dude, she

won't friend me on Facebook," and the other guys are responding with things like, "That's not right, kid. She don't want no part of your junk. That's all."

Mom two-thumb-types a message to someone on her phone, but she looks up in a panic. "Oh great," she says. "Stac just told me that Fox already has the Johnson murder for sweeps. Now what am I gonna do? I need something big!" She's all flustered and dewy looking. Getting red, too.

"I don't get it, Mom. You freak about sweeps every year, and isn't it, like in the summer?"

"Hell yeah I freak," she snaps, and takes a frantic sip of iced tea. "That's what measures our ratings. Pays my salary. Keeps me on board. My contract just so happens to be up in August and if I don't pull something big," she smacks the table with her hands, "then I'm gonna get canned. I'll be in Dubuque, Iowa before you know it, reading the freakin' crop report." Her head is back down and she types something else into her phone's keypad.

"Right," I say, now suddenly the parent. "I'm sure something huge will happen between now and July. You have, I dunno, three months. A lot can happen, ma."

"Oh God, but I've gotta get something now. What am I going to present at the planning meeting? I need something huge." A baby giggles from a table in the corner of the room. Her parents coo back and lock hands with each other.

Mom sighs. "I'm sorry, baby. This isn't your problem. I mean, if I don't work in this town anymore, it's no biggie, right?! You'll be fine if I make, say, one-hundred thousand less." She's half-sarcastic half-sincere…I think.

"Money's not everything, Mom." I agree.

She reaches over to touch my hand while her blinged-out bracelet shines from her wrist. "Nope. Nothing at all, Tirzah."

By the time my train gets in and I make it back home, it's already eleven. Lying on my bed, I fall in and out of sleep, sick to my stomach thinking about Heidi and JC. Sometimes I hate being alone. I think too much.

Then Hair Pie barges in my door.

"Ya gonna pay the electric bill this month sleepy?" He smacks the back of my head causing my vision to get all blurry. "Turn off your lights when you go to bed, turd."

"I'm still awake, ass eater."

"You look like you're half-dead."

"Bite me, and close the door on your way out, would you?"

Hair Pie swings his fist at me in a mock upper cut, "Gladly," he says, and the door slams behind him shaking my mini basketball net.

"Jerk!" I yell, but know it's a lame attempt to tell him off. My pillow feels much better the second time around, and I bury my face in it.

The next morning, the sun brushes my face just around the same time that music from my alarm clock blares in my room. My heart pumps in anticipation of our game.

I check myself in the mirror and notice the red under my eyes. My raccoon reflection kills the sing-song feeling I had a moment ago. Maybe if I grew my hair past my shoulders, maybe then I'd look better.

"Tirzah," my father calls from beyond my door, "Are you up?"

I meet him face to face in the doorway. "Almost game time, sunshine," he says.

"Morning, Dad. Just lemme get dressed, please."

"I don't know why you only give yourself five minutes to get ready for a game."

"Four, since the time you've been standing here," I say, smirking.

When the door closes, I head for the closet. Standing on my tip-toes, I grab for my silver Nike shoebox. I take four large rectangles of gauze and the white roll of surgical tape and stand in front of the mirror. I form a flat patch with two pieces of gauze and hold them against my breast with my left hand. My thumb presses the tape against my skin, and I yank at the roll, pulling as tightly as I can with my right hand, reaching around my back until I hear a pop in my shoulder. My left hand takes over and pulls the rest of the tape around my back, under my armpit, and back to my breast. I do the same thing on the right side.

The duct tape roll looks like it's almost out, only a nickel-thick, but I use whatever I can. I pull two long strips of tape off and lay them on top of the gauze. I slide a tank top over my head and over that, a long sleeve white shirt, and finally my jersey. In the mirror, there are no bumps or lumps on my chest. It's flat and perfect and I wish Heidi were in my room with me so she could see that I was so much more than JC.

5.

Later that afternoon, after I blocked nearly twenty balls from making it past me and the girls from St. Viader cried over their zero goals, I pull into Heidi's driveway and wait. Her dad takes his stance in the bay window, staring at me in my car in his driveway. I get out.

Inside, Heidi's brothers are playing golf on Wii. Hamid swings like there's an invisible club between his arms, and lets go. He says something I can't understand. His younger brother laughs.

I slip my shoes off at the door and stand in the entrance, waiting for her father to invite me in. He comes down the stairs. The sounds from his Qur'an recitation CD are echoing from upstairs.

He checks out my outfit—paint-stained pants and an old goalie jersey. "Where are you two going?"

I rehearse my lines in my head. "The movies. To see that one chick flick, oh, I don't remember the name of it." And I don't.

"Uh-huh." He rubs his eyebrows with the fingers of his

right hand in a rhythmic motion, back and forth, back and forth. "Just you two? You're not going with a larger group."

"Nope. Just us." I smile, and breathe deep as I see Heidi coming down the stairs in a black turtle neck and black pants. The Qur'anic performer's chanting still plays from the speakers somewhere upstairs. It's this beautiful voice, raising and lowering, loud and soft, saying words that sound so strong and beautiful. With the music playing, Heidi looks like some Muslim princess in American clothes. My heart thumps two loud beats.

Mr. Chaudary mumbles something to Heidi, and repeats it in English. "Those clothes, they just show every part of the body. Why don't you dress like our Blakean girl here? Wear more loose fitting garments? Why must you wear these revealing outfits?"

"Dad, please," Heidi says, "I'm wearing a turtleneck and pants. The only skin you can see is on my wrists and face. That's it. Now please, Dad, we can't be late."

"Sure you can." His hands are on his hips, pushing his stomach out farther than normal, accentuating its womb-like shape.

"Ho-hoooo! First place again, suckas!" Hamid shouts from across the room, playing his game. He dances with his legs and arms, around his sitting brother. "Lahoooosah!"

Mr. Chaudary shifts gears and turns away from us to celebrate. "That's my son!" He shouts. "A technological genius!"

Mrs. Chaudary scuffs her slippers on the wood floor and hugs Heidi. "Alright, my dear, enjoy yourself. You too,

Tirzah. We'll see you both back here by 10:30."

"Thanks, Mrs. C.," I say, and lower my head, thinking about Heidi going out with JC.

"You girls be careful," he adds, "I worry about you both out late at the movies. You never know who's there. Just be careful."

"We'll be fine, baba." Heidi kisses her father and mother.

What if JC doesn't get her back to my house in time?

Heidi turns down the radio in the car. "K. Listen. I told my p's that you'll have me home by ten-thirty—the usual—so I'll have JC bring me to your house by ten-fifteen." She's putting on dark plum colored lip-gloss. Her lips getting bigger and shinier and yummier by the second.

"Shouldn't you just have him bring you back by ten or something? I mean, what if you guys are late. Then I'm the one who your parents are gonna hate."

She flips the visor closed. "Tirz, seriously, it'll be fine." She puts her hand on my wrist while it's still on the steering wheel. I move it so it's on the center console, enjoying this moment where she's holding my arm.

"I just worry about you. I mean, are you sure you really want to go out with JC and not someone, I don't know, nicer?" I make a right turn on Forest Avenue and slow down when I see JC's car already parked in my driveway. It's one of those sleazy eighties cars that he's pimped out with faux fur seats and pillows in the backseat.

"Gah! He's already here!" Heidi checks the mirror again. She's still beautiful. "OK. So, don't forget, if my parents call your cell phone I'm just in the bathroom or something and then you call me and then I'll call them. Got it?"

"Got it," I grumble as we pull in my driveway. She's opening the door when I say, "Bye."

"Thanks! Love you!"

I'm nervous on the couch. It's 10:40 and Heidi hasn't called. Her parents are gonna call any minute now. I just know it. Some horror flick is on where everyone's turned into a vampire-zombie except this one guy. There are three Pringles left; I've eaten the entire can and I'm ready to eat more—anything to get my mind off Heidi and why she's not calling—when the phone rings. I jump because it's this really freaky part of the movie when this guy is searching for his dog in a dark building and you just know the vampire-zombie-people are going to eat him.

Heidi sounds messed up when she says hi. "Tirz, babe, you gotta come get me. I'm, um, yeah. I'm, um, seeing bunnies and they're jumping through the yard. And the big bunny wants to get me. He's evil with big scary eyes that pulsate when they look at me and—" she barfs. I can hear everything. The splatters. The hurls. And I'm freaking out because I have no idea if she's okay or where she is or where JC is, for that matter.

"Heidi?" I turn down the TV so all I can see is the guy in the dark and the small ray from his flashlight, and pulsating hollow bodies.

"…" I hear tons of talking and a really loud vintage Beatles song in the background.

"Heidi, are you there?" The barfing stops.

"Yep. Right here."

"Where are you?"

"Some party on Jefferson. I don't know, one of JC's friends." I grab my keys and open the garage door. "Dad, I'll be right back!" I shout upstairs. He mumbles 'alright' and I close the door.

6.

Jefferson is lined with cars on both sides of the street. I recognize most of them from the school lot. It's hard to tell which house has the party; they all have their outside lights on. But as I drive, I can see shadows of a crowd masked by drapes in a bay window of a small ranch. There's nowhere to park, so I pull in the driveway, my car still tailing in the street. I don't care. I just want Heidi out of there.

I push the door open without knocking. People are stuck in close-talking twosomes, laughing and gazing. On the couch, a girl's skirt is hiked up past her underwear as she rides some guy. Their faces are mashed together in hungry madness.

I can't find JC anywhere, but there's a guy named Rock that I know from class, standing in the kitchen, talking inches from another guy's face. Rock's eyes look like they're bulging out of his head. "Where's Heidi?" I ask, swaying back and forth in a panic.

"Upstairs, I think," Rock says, "somewhere with JC."

"A'ight. Thanks." We slap fives and I find the stairs.

Heidi is at the top. Half asleep, half awake.

"What happened?!" I ask, pushing the sweaty ringlets of hair from her forehead.

"Special K. I took a little and I don't know I'm not sure what really happened, but then I lost JC and panicked. Frickin' fell into a total K-hole. It was like I wasn't gonna live or something. I thought I was gonna die. Then I barfed and saw bunnies. Barfed again. And now I'm finally starting to feel normal, but shit, still not really normal. Like all cold and freaky and shaky." I lift the top of her body from the shaggy carpet. The cat tranquilizer has her all limp. Her shirt drenched in sweat, I lean her in my lap.

"You can't go home like this. There's no way. I'm taking you to my house." She closes her eyes. A smile forms on her sleepy lips.

"Heidi, you've gotta get up. Let's go, OK?" She shakes her head as if I dumped cold water on her.

"Right, OK. Yep! Let's gOOOooooo!" Her voice is cute and crackly, loud and then soft. I lift her to her feet, and she locks her arms around my waist.

She opens her hand. JC's one-inch plastic monkey is wedged between her fingers and sweaty palm. "Look. Funky Fresh." She lets out a long sigh. "He freakin' gave me Funky Fresh."

"Yup. Yeah that's so thoughtful of him..." I wanna throw the little speck of a monkey over the stairwell, but she'd probably jump after it. Alright. It's kind of cute, sitting with his head propped up on his arms, and his little monkey feet crossed behind him.

Heidi kisses Funky Fresh, and its head sinks in the circle of space between her lips. Then she puts the monkey in her pocket and pats the outside of her pants to make sure he's still there.

We take the stairs one at a time, her body heavy and lazy against mine.

The door is just a few feet from the bottom of the stairs, but I can't leave. Not without finding JC. Where the hell is he?

"I'm gonna put you in the car, then I'm gonna sneak back inside for one second to use the bathroom."

Heidi shakes her head in agreement.

After I lean the passenger seat back and lay her body onto the cold seat, I strut back into the house. Back to Rock. "Dude, where's JC?"

"Shit, like I said, thought he was with Heidi."

"Nope. He wasn't. And she's totally wacked right now. Says she took some K. Sound about right?"

The pupils of his eyes are huge and black and beaming at me. He bites his bottom lip. "Probably right. But she wanted it. I mean, she said she's done it before and she'd be fine. Everyone else was fine on it."

"Alright. I'll catch ya later." I walk around the corner, to a part of the house I hadn't been through before and find an open door that leads down to a basement. The lights are off, but I smell cigarette smoke. A lit cherry glows like a beady red eye in a dark cave. Candlelight outlines a blanketed mass near the bottom of the stairs.

"JC, you down there?" I step down slowly.

"Who wants to know?" He calls out. When I reach the bottom of the stairs, I find him on the floor with a blanket and a candle and a half-naked girl. "Shit!" He shouts and throws the blanket over the girl, but not before I see her huge tits and two rolls of extra skin on her stomach. She buries her face in his bare arm.

"What about Heidi? I found her all wowed out at the top of the stairs. By herself. What happened?"

He scrambles for his pants. "I found her making out with Chris James, and I was like, what? When she saw me she started yellin' for me to go away. Said I was frickin' Bugs Bunny."

"And you left her?"

"Sure as shit. She looked like she was going to kick my ass. Later, some chick was takin' care of her in the bathroom. All the puke was makin' me sick. They kept screaming at me to go away." He stands up while the grungy girl puts her shirt on underneath the blanket. "So I did."

"You're such an asshole!" I leave to head back up the stairs. Who knows what JC's on or what he's capable of doing to me. He follows and grabs me, locking me in his arms so my stomach is touching his. "Listen you bitch, or whatever you are," his breath smells like my medicine cabinet, "don't tell anyone about this, you hear me, or I'll be sure to tell everyone about your little secret." I wonder how he knows about me, like, when would he have had the chance to read my mind. Or maybe he's some freaky mind-reader.

"I know you've been skating in the city. Acting like a

dude. I got friends who skate at that park. Tellin' me that some new guy from Trinity's comin' around like Hawk, making everyone look bad. They like you, though. Don't get me wrong."

My heart is racing. "Wait. What? How do you know that's me?" How'd he know what I do in the city at my mom's?

"Let's just say that I know. And if you don't want word gettin' back to the boys in the city that you're actually a chick and not a dude, then I suggest you keep your mouth shut about whatever you might think you saw down here." I press my lips close together. I'm not gonna argue with a drunk asshole who's probably all messed up on pills. Plus, I remember one guy was filming with his pocket cam, but I didn't think anything of it at the time. Fucking technology. Anyone ever thought of just living life and not recording it for the world to see? Like living the life that's really there instead of making one up for YouTube.

I run up the stairs and out of that nightmare.

I wish I could tell Heidi what happened, but she's passed out in a ball with the seatbelt strap behind her back. I wish she could see my tears, my pain, my problems, but there's no time for me right now when she's the one who needs to come down from her high.

"Mr. Chaudary?" I say when he answers the phone. Heidi is snoring on my bed. "Um, this is Tirzah, and Heidi fell asleep in my car on the way home, so, like, would you mind, sir, if she spent the night?" He breathes heavily into the phone, the exhale making a cackling noise in my ear.

"I tried calling Hafsa several times! Why didn't she answer?"

I pull Heidi's phone from her small purse. Eleven missed calls from home. Shit. "Um, the movie was really loud, and it looks like she turned the ringer off. I'm sorry, Mr. C., she just got so tired and fell asleep. I mean, she'll be fine. I'll bring her home first thing in the morning." He mumbles something that I can't understand, to his wife, I'm guessing.

Then Mrs. Chaudhary gets on the phone. "Tirzah, dear, what has happened?" I retell the story. My stomach gurgles and an empty burp escapes, like my body just can't handle lying.

She interrupts. "Oh, I don't know, is your father there? Can I speak to him please?"

With the phone in my hand, I find dad in bed reading, and whisper what's going on—well basically what I told Heidi's parents—and he handles the rest.

Back in my room, I change into my pajamas, watching my body in the mirror—my B cup breasts and soft stomach, this body that just doesn't seem right for me.

With my t-shirt and flannel pants on, I slide next to Heidi on the bed. My body tight behind hers. My legs bend where hers bend. My feet underneath hers. I rest my face in her back and begin to fall asleep when she turns toward me. Our noses touch. She presses her lips against mine. I smell the sweat from her upper lip. I move my lips from hers and instead place them on the spot above her left eyebrow until I fall asleep.

Sunday morning, Heidi and I meet her dad at the museum on his lunch break. She thinks this is the way to get back on his good side after last night by showing interest in his work.

We check in at the front, and the receptionist rings Heidi's dad. Minutes later he's down in the great lobby, his arms outspread for hugs us. "Oh, girls, such a wonderful treat. Joining your old baba on his lunch break." He checks his watch. The digital face says 12:12.

"Ahhh, perfect balance. Twelve-twelve," he says. "Just like life should be—balanced—one side equaling out the other side." He points toward the right corner of the museum. "Has our favorite Blakean girl seen the butterfly habitat yet?"

"Never. But I would love to see it, sir."

He pats my back. "That's my girl."

We pass a large mammoth model, and walk beneath its massive, outstretched tusks.

"Hafsa, you were quite tired last night, huh? Fell asleep?"

Heidi wraps her arm around her father's back. "Yep." She gulps. "The movie was kind of boring and made me sleepy, baba. I'm sorry." He sighs before opening a heavy set of engraved doors.

We enter the greenhouse. Bright plants line small paths. Butterflies dance around, their wings flapping in beats.

"Wow, this is beautiful," I say, watching gold and brown butterfly rest on a tree. The right wing perfectly reflects the left; five dots at the bottom, two odd-shaped ovals, a black outline meeting in the center. This is paradise: a large fountain spills in the center of the greenhouse; hedges cut in mazes; color and fragrance and clean air.

Mr. Chaudary walks with his hands behind him, fingers locked, shoulders back. "The most beautiful insects, yes, but with one of the shortest life spans." Heidi opens her hand as a colorful butterfly dances before us. It lands on her shoulder, flaps its wings as she looks at me. Our eyes meet and lock. There is so much I want to say, maybe quote the Keats letter that Mr. Kipp read in English class. I would live only three days if it meant spending every moment with her. But she'd totally think I was tripping.

After a tour, Mr. Chaudhary pulls up his sleeve to check his watch. "Alright, girls, I must get back to work, but you two enjoy yourselves." He kisses Heidi's forehead. "Stay well, my sweet." And then he taps my shoulder. "You two enjoy. God is surely great." He opens his arms to motion at the beautiful surroundings. "Gardens and flowing waters—just paradise."

"Thank you, Mr. C."

Once the heavy doors close, Heidi and I face each other, meeting eyes. It's like the rest of the world doesn't exist. Only us.

I spot a bench near a taller tree. "Let's chill for a bit. You're probably totally tired still, huh?"

"I'm alright. Just a little out of it," Heidi says, and we sit together, thighs touching. A family of four passes by: a baby in a stroller, an older boy, and two hand-holding parents. They smile and continue on the path.

"He's such an ass. Leaving me alone like that."

I shake my head and wait until the family is out of sight.

Then, I slide my hand next to Heidi's. "You know, maybe there are other people out there for you besides JC," I say.

Heidi smirks while a butterfly lands on the bench arm, but it leaves within a few seconds.

She pulls Funky Fresh from her jeans pocket, and holds him up on her palm. "You hear that, little man. Tirzah thinks I can do better than your papa." She puts the monkey up to her ear. "Nawww. Ya think? He did look like a long-eared cartoon bunny last night. But you think I can do better than Bugs?"

I tuck a piece of her hair behind her ear, admiring the perfect shine on the bump above the circular hole, wishing I could kiss the softest part by her silver earring. "You askin' me or the monkey?"

She holds Funky Fresh between her thumb and first finger. "You."

"Hmmm. Me. Like you're askin' me, or it *is* me."

"Uh-huh."

I put my right hand up to meet her left hand and lock my pinky with her pinky. We move our hands up and down, turning and flapping our fingers like the wings of a butterfly. Together, we raise our arms up, watching our manmade monarch dance.

She drops her hand and rubs my leg. "You know, if you weren't you and I wasn't me, I think I'd want to spend my life with you. If only for three days."

"You remember that letter, too? I was gonna say something when we got here, but didn't want you to think I was all Bob Marley."

She laughs. "No, it's perfect. Just perfect, this idea that butterflies only live for a few days and the rest of the time they spend in the body of a nubby caterpillar. So much time preparing for just a few days of beautifulness."

"Beautifulness? Niiiice. But wait. You've totally changed the subject. I mean, we were talking about JC and then you said 'you,' like I'm better than JC, but did you mean that?" Then I hate myself for saying that, like how does that happen? Usually there's some sort of delay between what my brain is thinking and what my mouth is saying, but this time the whole method of transport got all fucked up.

The silence kills me until Heidi says, "You have no idea what I'm thinking, do you?"

"I think I do."

She moves her hand a little higher on my leg. I breathe deep.

"But why JC?"

"Cuz he's not what I'm supposed to have. Because I can't have him. I can never be with someone like him. You know I'll end up with some Bangladeshi guy—the son of one of my dad's friends or something. A good Muslim husband. Never a JC."

We get up, together, and follow the path toward the maze of sculpted hedges. "I don't know if I can handle this anymore, Heidi. I mean, I like you more than friends. You're someone I could spend forever with, and it's hard knowing—"

She stops me and holds my hands. "I just haven't figured it all out, yet. I mean, I'm really attracted to guys like JC, but it's fun to play around with you, too." I drop my hands. I don't want to be Heidi's tease. Seriously?

"Going to your mom's tonight?" She asks. Totally changing the subject—again.

"Yeah. Train leaves at three. She wants to have dinner at that place where they kiss her ass before she goes to work."

"Dude, you make it out to be so bad. Your mom's a freakin' news anchor. That's awesome!" Heidi stops to read the plaque in front of a wiry-looking bush.

"She sold herself out for that job. Gave up her family and all."

"Tirzah, seriously, get over it. They divorced 'cuz of a gazillion things, not that job." I follow Heidi toward the door and take one last deep breath before leaving so I can capture the smells.

The museum is loud and we are lost amongst a group of tourists, staring at the rings of a petrified tree.

"The tomb!" Heidi shouts. "We've still got half an hour to see the tomb!" She pulls my head and skips across the hall toward the ancient Egypt exhibit.

The sculpted walls are narrow, leading us into a dark tunnel. We are alone in this fake underground maze, surrounded by dark painted cement and signs dictating the insides of glass cases. After looking at jewels and fossilized dead cats, we're in a dark space, following cement imprints of barefoot markings, leading the way to the pharaoh's tomb.

We stop in front of a wide-eyed mummified woman surrounded by gold bracelets, plates, and a carved vase. Heidi wraps her arms around me from behind. She puts her lips up to my ear. "When I die, I think you should wrap me in bubble wrap, and cover me in all your bling. Give me Cocoa Puffs, cups, and plates, too, in case I get hungry." She laughs quietly in my ear and the heat from her mouth makes my body tingle.

"I'll be sure to throw a frozen pizza in your coffin, too. And some Twizzlers."

"Feelin' the posthumous love already."

I turn my head so our lips are separated by a few inches. She drops from her tiptoes and nudges me to continue through the tomb.

7.

I jump on my board and roll down the half-pipe feeling the strong city wind. Up on the platform, I check the other skaters. A guy in a black sweatshirt with white diamonds clips his board just before hitting the top. He gets all pissed off and walks up the rest of the ramp towards me.

"I just can't get it today." He looks at me. "You new here?"

"Yeah, my first time at this park." My voice a little deeper.

"Dude, what's your name again?" He sticks his hand out to smack mine. Dude? He called me dude, or is he just sayin' that?

"Troy." I answer. Shit, I forgot to lower my voice. My heart races, and I clear my throat. "I'm Troy." Much better. I bump knuckles with the guy and tuck my long bangs underneath the brim of my baseball cap.

"Costa," he says, "C's fine." He drops his board at his feet and skates to the other side. I follow, holding my legs just like he did. Wide. Heavy. We go on like this for a while:

he skates; I skate. Each time I'm more confident. Free. But we don't say much. It's more about the sport and less about talking, and I'm totally fine with that.

"You've got some skills, man. How long you been skatin'?"

"Since sixth grade. You?"

"Few years."

I jump back on my board and fly up the side of the half-pipe, catching air, grabbing my board with my hands, and hitting the wood again.

A metal guitar song rages from my cell phone. "Hey."

" . . . "

"Yeah, OK, I'm coming."

I skate over to C. "Gotta go. Mom's buggin' me."

"Catch ya next time." C slaps hands with me again. I punch his knuckles and quickly walk around the corner—not sure if Mom is on the hunt to find me.

"There you are Tirzah!" My mother calls out from across the four-lane street. Her hug takes my breath away, her peach and rose smell reminding me of happy times when she baked pies and decorated with cheap crafty stuff.

"Do you want to change out of your uniform?" She inspects my unshaven calves and my long shorts. "I've got reservations at that quaint little French place on Michigan Avenue."

"This isn't my soccer uniform, Mom," I sigh. "I'm fine, right?" Mom dusts my shoulder off and quickens her pace. I follow her shiny black heels up the escalator.

A model-like hostess whispers something to a waiter and greets Mom and me with a smile. "Good afternoon, Mrs.

Maxon. We've got your favorite table ready for you right against the windows."

I slide on the leather booth and gaze out onto the sidewalk, watching people the size of mice hustle in and out of stores.

"Isn't this just the best view of Michigan Avenue?" Mom squeaks.

"It's great, Mom."

A tall, tanned waiter is at the end of our table. "Mrs. Maxon, will you be having your usual?" He winks.

"Of course, dear." She grins as if hungry for the waiter and not lunch.

"And how about your…" He pauses.

"Daughter."

"Yes, your daughter, what can I get you?" He pulls his glance from Mom to address me. I nervously flip through the menu with French foods and fancy names.

"Do you have burgers?" My voice is quiet.

Waiter-guy grins at me like I'm a toddler. "Suuuuuure. You can special order a burger. What kind of cheese would you like on top? Gorgonzola, Muenster, smoked-apple Gouda?" The names sound like towns from history class.

"How 'bout good 'ole processed American cheese please." I return his child-like smile.

Mom pats my hand. "What's in your bag dear? It looks like you brought a small chair with you."

"My skateboard, Mom. I brought my skateboard."

"I didn't know girls did that kind of thing." Mom looks disgusted.

"I found a skate park online, right around the corner from your condo. I might go back later if you don't mind." What's weird is that I'm always at the skate park and this is the first time she's asking. Mom glances around the room, probably looking to see who notices her, and sets her eyes back on me. Uninterested.

"Fine. That sounds alright, I guess. I just thought we could, maybe, go shopping or something. You know, I'm not going to see you in two weeks. I'll be in San Francisco on business." Right. Business. With the same guy she's been doing business with since the divorce.

I pull a piece of bread from the basket in front of me and wipe the sesame seeds from its crust. "Not tonight," I say. "Go ahead, Ma, we'll hang out later. K?"

Back at Mom's I've spent two hours playing Wii when she returns from shopping with four bags filled with clothes from the top department stores.

"Oooooh. Wait 'til you see what I found you, Tirz, just wait!" She throws her keys on the glass kitchen table and pulls out shirts and jeans with pink, sparkly crap.

I pause the game. "Go try them on, dear?"

"Later, K?" My face gets hot and I wonder what happened between the time that Mom and I were so close and going on walks and playing at the park, to now, where she can't see that I DON'T wear pink clothes and sparkly stuff. I plot out a way that I can try the clothes on and pretend that they just don't fit me. But someday I'm gonna have to tell her the truth.

And then my mouth moves before my head can tell it to stop. "Why are you pushing your style on me, anyway?" I snap. "I mean, why are you always asking me what I'm wearing, and dusting off my shoulders, and looking at my outfits like they're just so—uh—unacceptable?" I stand up, so the only thing dividing us is the couch. And I'm glad it's there because I'm so pumped right now that I almost wanna get in her face.

Mom looks mortified—mouth wide open, eyes bugging like a squeezed frog. "Seriously, Tirzah. You're going to talk to me that way after all I've done for you. After I gave birth to you and raised you."

"And left!" I shout. "You don't even know who I am anymore, Mom."

She's shaking and stops to take a deep breath. "Alright. I left. Yes. But with many reasons, Tirzah. But that's not what this is about. I just wish you'd dress better and clean yourself up. Maybe guys would notice you then. I don't think I've ever seen you date anyone. Have I?"

"No. I don't wanna date. No time for drama." I'm half-ready to just tell her that I don't like guys, but she looks like she's on the verge of some major catastrophic breakdown and I'm not gonna be the one to push her over the cliff.

At the point when things cool down and we're ready to take some time to talk and hang out, her phone rings. She checks to see who's calling, and opens the phone. "Hey, baby," she coos into the phone, turns her back to me, and heads into her bedroom. The door closes.

Nothing has changed. Mom can never just live in the

moment. She's always letting other things get in the way. The phone. Her job. News stories. Her boyfriend. Never, ever, ever me.

Later that night when Mom is asleep, I try to call Heidi. Her phone is off. I send her an e-mail and wait by the computer, hoping she's there at the same moment and can send me a message right back.

Nothing.

I miss her and want to hear her voice. Want to know that everything's OK since the museum. I worry that her Dad found JC's number on her phone from the so-called movie night. I feel sad and lonely and sick. I want to laugh with her and talk about nothingness, pretend we're gangstas and type text messages in slang. I want Monday to be here so I can see her again, but the time is going by so slowly and she is in the suburbs and I am in the city. Maybe I could take a train out tonight and go see her. Climb up her deck and knock on her window.

There are still no messages in my inbox when I lay on my overly stuffed pillows, like the Princess and the Pea, only I'm the prince on a pile of pillows. I close my eyes and pretend that Heidi is lying next to me, rubbing my hand on the soft comforter. I pretend her leg is wrapped around me like it was last weekend. If I focus hard enough, I can almost feel her skin next to mine.

8.

I'm watching the outline of Ryan Connesty's head, the clean haircut, the smooth skin, big shoulders. His legs are wide spread and he hunches over to take notes. I move my left foot to mimic his stance, loosening my shoulders to match his posture.

Skye flicks my neck. "Sit still, would ya, I can't see the whiteboard." I turn around to meet her eyes, which are glazed over as she gleams at me. I put my hands up and look at her, mouthing the word, "what?" and replace my toughness with a smile. Hiding my teeth under my lips so Kipp doesn't think we're talking.

In the hallway, JC slams me against the wall. "What up, Maxon?" He says, looking in my eyes like he's gonna kill me. He could.

I fight everything inside that wants to tell him to fuck off, and instead I say, "Nothin', dude, nothin's up. Everythin's fine."

As he leans in close to my face, I can smell milk and something like cinnamony granola on his breath. "You're looking mighty butch this morning. Getting' your guy on, huh?"

I meet his glance, his pupils getting larger and smaller, pulsating like mad. I just stare back, saying nothing.

He looks around the hallway. A crowd has gathered, waiting for a fight.

"You sure 'bout that?" He shouts.

Again, I stay silent.

JC slides his hand up the painted brick wall, his fingers brushing against my side. I inch away so I'm no longer pinned in a spot that I can't break free from.

Skye approaches. She tickles JC's side. "Get a room you two!" She says, and I escape from JC completely, holding Skye from behind so she's in between JC and me.

"We were just talking, that's all," JC says.

"Right. I mean, aren't you dating Heidi or something?" Skye asks.

"No. No way," he repeats. "We're just friends, ya know." His face freezes like he has temporary paralysis from lying.

"Whatev, maybe I heard wrong." Skye turns from JC and stands close to me. "Catch ya later, K?" She says to him.

He's sipping water from the fountain. "Yep."

When JC's halfway down the hall, I say to Skye, "You have no idea how you just saved me." Her eyes widen as I tell her the whole story about the skanky girl and JC in the basement. But I stop when I see Heidi at our lockers.

"We just saw your boyfriend," Skye sings, as if I didn't just tell her that JC wanted to beat the shit out of me.

"No way! Is he still mad at me? I mean, did you get to ask him?" She brushes her hair. Loose strands fall from the brush to the floor.

Skye looks at the clock on the wall. "Shit! I've gotta go to P-E. You two work it out, K?" And she takes off running down the hall.

"Mad at you?" I ask Heidi. "You've got his pet monkey, right? He didn't ask for it back, did he?"

"Still got him," she says, pulling the plastic monkey from the hand pockets of her hoodie.

"You gave the monkey a necklace?" I take a closer look at the gold twist tie wrapped around its neck. There's a tiny yellow piece of construction paper hanging from the middle with the letters FF.

"Funky Fresh needed some bling." She kisses the monkey and holds it up to my lips so I have to kiss it, too. "Tirz, JC didn't do anything wrong at that party. It was me. I was the idiot who wanted to try the K. I'm the one who got all fucked up and thought he was a killer bunny. Shit. What was I thinkin' taking cat tranquilizer? I mean, seriously, what was I thinking?"

"I don't know. You sure he didn't make you take it?"

"No, he wouldn't even do it. I was already smashed on whiskey, and thought it'd be fun to try it. Rock and those guys kept laughing and dancing, and I thought that's what'd happen to me."

Her forehead crinkles up. "Why are you looking at me like that, you crazy bitch?" She grabs my chin and fakes a kiss. I resist. No kiss. No truth. If I ever told Heidi about the other girl and JC found out he'd have every guy at school pounding my ass.

"No reason," I muster, and check the clock. "The second bell's gonna ring."

She blows an air-kiss at me and slams her locker with her foot. As she turns the corner, JC finds her, and puts his hand in her back pocket. I watch them walk together and swallow the guilt in my throat.

I can't go to American studies. I want to read more about Jane Addams and her plight to save the poor, but I'm stuck in this lump. Heidi's still with JC, and I'm still alone. The thought of JC touching Heidi again makes me sick. I have to tell her what he did. I couldn't live with myself if he hurt her.

I make my way toward Rip's office, hoping he'll just let me hide out in there and get my shit together. He's cool like that. Usually.

When I get into the gym, there's a light on in Rip's office. He's sitting at his desk, reading something online.

"Hey, can I hang here for a bit?" I ask. "Having a tough day."

Rip looks at my face, his lips form a sympathetic frown. "Sure, kid. No prob. What's up?"

I sit in the hard chair next to his desk. "Just some prick won't leave me alone. And I know this guy is no good, but there's something about him that makes me think he's really alright on the inside. But he thinks he has to be all tough and shit on the outside."

Rip wipes his mouth with his hand, like he's coaxing it to say the right words. Then he says, "I think I know who you're talking about. And yeah, he seems like a prick, but there is something cool about that guy. I just haven't figured out what. Maybe at home he's one of those kids who is good to his mother. Like he probably takes care of her like crazy."

And then I let out a laugh when a thought comes to my head. "Yeah, maybe his dad's like a troll or something who can't leave the house and his mom fell in love with a troll and married him and they have three troll babies, but JC isn't a troll." Now I have the giggles.

Rip laughs. "You're so goofy, Maxon. I think we'd better take you to the school psychologist and have that brain of yours checked out." He nudges my shoulder, and hunches his back over, scrunches his face, and growls.

I growl back.

We're silent for a minute, and Rip goes back to the computer, skimming through news stories. I get closer and read, too.

He scrolls past a headline that says, "NCAA Changes Policy for Transgender Athletes."

"Hey, go back, would ya?" I ask. "Go back that NCAA story."

Rip runs his finger on the top of the mouse while the computer screen page moves back to the story. He gets out of his chair and motions for me to sit.

From the article, it looks like a basketball player who was born as a guy but identifies as a girl is able to play on a Division I women's team. And there are rules and regs that protect her.

I stop scrolling through the article when I reach the bottom, when Rip says. "That's amazing. I mean, colleges would've never done something like that when I was in school. Maybe there were athletes that we knew were not totally masculine, but they would've never been able to switch genders and play on the women's team."

It's like I've just found an article that said, "Tirzah Maxon's Life Gets a Helluva Lot Better, Starting Today."

"What does this mean, Rip?" I lean in and scroll back up to the top of the article, checking to see if it's some kind of joke from the Onion's website. But it's the sports section of The Times. I ask Rip, "Are they saying that if you identify as a different gender that you can actually become that gender and still play sports?"

Rip reads through the story again. "Yeah. I think so. Kinda amazing." He looks at me, attempting to read me, it seems. Then he checks his watch. "Bell's gonna ring soon, kiddo. Better get to your next class. I'll send a message to the office and say you spent the hour in my office. But you can't stay all day."

"Gottcha," I say, not really hearing what he's telling me because I'm so stoked about the article. I glance back at the headline on the screen. "Hm." So maybe all that role playing like I'm a guy in the city, maybe I can actually be who I know I am. Is that even possible?

9.

The morning of Regionals, Dad is pacing outside my room, my cleats and uniform dangling from his arms. "Hurry, sweetheart, your bus leaves the school in ten minutes!"

I throw some shorts and t-shirts, underwear, sports bras, and socks in my duffle bag and lace up my shoes.

"Ready!" I shout. Dad lets out a deep sigh and heads down the hall toward the garage.

"You excited?" He asks, then starts the car. "Big game! This is it, kid, Regionals. Remember to tell the scouts that they must talk to me first. I'll be sure to set up appointments for you, but I don't want you making any promises. College is a big step, and I'm sure we can get you in the door at one of the best if we just play our cards right.

"I've put a good word in with the sports director at Illinois University." Dad is an I-U junkie: on the board, taught there a couple summers, swears that's where I'll get in.

"Got it, Dad. But I still don't get why you can't come this weekend." Dad pulls into the school driveway. The bus is already filled with the entire varsity girls' soccer team.

"Conference, kiddo. It's something we academics do to show each other how smart we are. Remember last summer when I wrote that Marxist piece on *Moll Flanders*. Well, I'm bringing Moll to Northwestern. Great school."

"Dad, seriously, snooze! Who still reads stuff from the Dark Ages?" I open the car door. He follows, and grabs my duffle bag from the trunk.

"Eighteenth-century, my dear—not the Dark Ages. Big difference." He kisses my nose. "Throw it out there, Tirzah. Use your head to keep that ball away," he says, and knocks gently on my skull.

"Love you!" I call out as I approach the sidewalk. "See you Sunday!"

"Love you!" He answers back and slides back into his car. From the rolled down window he shouts, "And don't forget to tell Coach Shoals I said hello!"

I feel a rush of nerves as our bus pulls into Northern Illinois University's parking lot, directly across from a large castle-like tower. A dozen other buses are lined up, while groups of players gather in the lot, holding bags and pillows, cleats and water bottles.

"We're staying in this campus hotel," Rip says, pointing toward a large brick building. "Let's file out and get settled, which should only take twenty-minutes or so. Then we'll head over to the field for warm-ups." He hands us each a folder as we pass him, walking in a sloppy line toward the building. "Check this folder for your room assignment and our schedule. We're the second game, so while the others are playing, we'll do our warm-ups and go over our plays again." He stops me. "This is it, Maxon." His smile is huge. "I just know something big's gonna happen today for you."

"Thanks, Coach, I'll try not to let you down. We've got this thing. Solid." I bump knuckles with Rip, while trying to hold my pillow in my underarm. It's an awkward knuckle-knock, but it works. Rip let's out a "huh!"

I glance down at the folder he's handed me, and on the front is a sticker that says "Roommate: Marisol Valdez, Room 219." I should have known better than to think he'd pair Heidi and me together.

When I get to my room, Sol is unpacking, tossing her stuff in drawers. "Hey, Tirz, kinda cool that we got paired up together, huh?" She opens a package of sweet Mexican candies and offers me some.

I grab a few. "No, yeah, this is totally a good thing," I'm kind of lying and half-wonder if she'd mind if I ask her to switch with Heidi. But I don't want to hurt her feelings. "Which bed do ya want?"

She shrugs her shoulders. "Doesn't matter."

I decide on the bed closer to the door so if I want to, I can sneak out easily while she's sleeping. Not that I will. But still.

I'm pulling on my shin guards when Rip calls out for us to gather outside. My stomach rumbles from nerves. I grab an apple from my bag and munch it on the way out in hopes that it'll calm my stomach.

Heidi catches me in the hall. "Skye and I are roommates.

63

I see you have Sol, huh?" She's got that look in her eyes. "Wanna switch. I mean, do you think Sol would room with Skye?" I don't know why Heidi teases me so badly, but there's no way I could room with her and not spend the night awake and wondering if I should try something.

"Sol won't want to switch. She's already staked out her bed, set up her laptop, and all that shit. We'll be fine." Heidi makes a sad face so the redness of the inside of her eyes shows.

"Stop with that face. You kind of look like an alien."

"Shut up!" She hits my arm then slides hers underneath mine and picks up speed in her walk, pulling me along with her. "This is your weekend, mama, and I want you to get sleep, anyways. We'll be fine where we are, right?" She bumps my hip with hers.

In a small field, outside the stadium, my soccer team forms a massive circle. We're all facing each other, jogging in place with our knees as high as they can go. My right knee is a little stiff, but I fight through my worrying about whatever damage it might have. Instead, I focus on our team and the sense of strength I get from just being a part of it.

"Break!" Rip shouts and we rush over to a spot in the grass where our water bottles are waiting. I bend down to stretch my legs, pulling my nose to my knee. The smell of grass and dirt pumps me up and puts me in the mood for a victory.

Three older guys are talking and laughing with each other off to the side of our group. They are scouts, I'm sure.

Rip whispers in my ear, "Go with I-U," before he walks me over to the group of adults.

"Here she is," Rip says, tapping my shoulder. A guy in an Illinois University windbreaker extends his hand.

"Tirzah Maxon? I'm Coach Shoals. Illinois University." We shake. I'm stuck staring at the stern look in his graying eyes.

When he let's go from our handshake, I pull away, respecting his lead. "Nice to meet you, Coach."

"Listen, we've been watching your tapes and if you play the way you've been, consistently blocking most, if not all of the goals, well then Ms. Maxon, we'd sure like to have you on our team once you finish high school." He looks toward Rip for reassurance.

"Oh, Maxon here won't let you down. She's a star, Coach. She's a star."

"I probably won't see you after the game, but we'll send you a letter later. It'll go over scholarship information and all the necessary paperwork. To be honest, we've never seen a girl play as tough as you." His comment doesn't sit right with me, but I brush the girl-thing off.

"Thanks again, Mr. Shoals, I hope I don't let you down."

Rip tugs at the whistle hanging on a string around his neck. "Now if you'll excuse me," Rip says to the coach and I. Then he blows the whistle. "Huddle up, girls, let's get ready to take this baby." There's a bunch of cheering before we gather in our circle, and I get that knotted feeling again in my stomach. This is huge. If I can block all of the goals, I will get to go to freakin' Illinois University. That's the last door I need opened so I can go on to play pro.

What's weird is that I just can't picture myself on some women's team for the rest of my life. That's like Edward hanging with humans and trying not to be a vampire. He's a vampire and nothing can change that, right? As much as he tries to hide it, he has vampire parts, not human parts. But what if Edward was born human but knew he was a vampire? And everything he did to try to be human didn't work, like he always knew he was someone he wasn't supposed to be. Nothing could hide it. As much as I try to hide it, I have girl parts and not guy parts. But if that one basketball player can change and play on the team she belongs on, then why can't I?

10.

Coach Shoals stalks me from the corner of my team's bench, jotting notes on a clipboard and typing something in his phone. I feel like some prized racecar in a showroom, on display, for sale. We're facing off with Mellor High when Luz snatches the ball from Mellor's forward, some tall-ass chick with spiked hair. I loosen up, watching the action from my goalie box. Like graceful giants, the girls pass the ball back and forth, moving seamlessly through Mellor's defense. Heidi's on the sideline, fists clenched, body moving right and left as she watches the ball on the field, like she's mirroring the players. They all seem to go together like one, moving the same and running the same, jumping the same and screaming the same.

Then there's me.

Alone.

Guarding.

Waiting.

As the ball heads toward my end of the field, I'm not so into guarding and waiting and being alone. I'm not so into this life of being a girl anymore. Coach Shoals watches and types, squinting at my lax stance in the box. The ball is getting closer, the graceful giants getting larger, and I'm still in my spot. Knees soft. Hands relaxed.

Mellor's forward kicks the ball at the corner of the box, and instead of diving like I always do, risking every bone in my body for that small ball, I put my leg out to stop it. Who cares if it goes in? This is just a girl's game. Why shouldn't I be graceful and aggressive at the same time? More careful and less deadly.

The buzzer sounds and the crowd cheers. Mellor's players bump chests, slap fives, and rejoice. Luz smacks the back of my head. "Maxon, what happened to you? Come on, you alright?" She shakes her head.

I feel like an ass. "I'm fine, Luz, my knee's killing me, though." Grabbing my knee, I flag Rip on the field. He looks like he's going to vomit from worry.

"Maxon, dude, what's going on? You alright?"

"My knee," I say, "It popped and, oh, I don't know, not doing well."

Rip looks back toward the bench at Shoals and our team, at Jazz, my backup goalie. "Want me to grab Jazz?"

"Mm-hm. Yeah. Probably," I muster, holding my knee for effect.

Rip wraps his arm around my back, and I lean on him for support. I hobble a little as we make our way toward the bench. Our fans cheer, happy that I got up.

Coach Shoals stands. "You alright, Tirzah?" His brows are all crinkled.

"Yeah, I think so. Just popped something, I think."

Shoals types something in his phone as our medic has me sit on the bench. She asks me a few questions and works with my leg, bending and straightening it super slowly.

Shoals hunches down near us and clears his throat. "Looks like I'm going to have to get going, Tirzah. Something unexpected, you know." He won't look at my eyes—only my knee.

"Take care of yourself, alright?" Shoals says. "Good luck with the rest of the tourney."

Rip shakes his hand; so do I. But there's something limp about his handshake, like he just can't wait to leave.

"Oh man," Rip says under his breath.

"What?" I ask.

"No, nothing, Maxon. Let's just work on getting you better." He flags Jazz over. "You're going in, alright? You've got this, Jazzy. Put up the iron gates. Let nothing through. You got this!" His voice gets louder and deeper.

Jazz pulls her leg behind her, stretching her tanned hamstring. "Rest up, Tirzah. I won't let you down, Coach. We got this!" She runs toward the goal, taking a spot near the front edge of the box. Bad spot. She's got too much space open behind her.

"Back it up!" I yell, pissed at myself for letting her take my place. She doesn't look my way. "Jazz! Back up!" I yell again, waving my hand, motioning for her to move backward. She still doesn't hear me. What was I thinking, giving up my spot?

By the end of the game, Jazz is virtually unscathed, barely sweaty, but still victorious. Our team pulls her from the goal, smothers her in hugs and celebrates her greatness. I stroll over to be a part of their celebration, but am a total outcast. My teammates see me, but they're just not so into me anymore. I let them down. And the worst part is I'm not even that injured. I was just having a moment.

Heidi's brothers approach as our team huddles in a victory hug. They stand to the side, watching.

In the distance, JC and Chris Jones are off by the concession stand, talking to some girls who are laughing and chewing on long Super Ropes. Heidi pulls out of our group huddle, still sweaty and ecstatic from our win, and shifts her eyes from the concession stand to her brothers.

"Shit!" She whispers in my ear. "When did JC get here? And my frickin' brothers. What the hell? I have, like, the worst luck ever!" Her sweaty face rests close to my cheek and I can feel her nose tickle my ear as she talks.

"Alright. Don't worry. There's a way to get around this." I glance at her brothers, who have now moved directly behind us.

"Hafsa," they call out. "…" I can't understand the rest. They sound happy, though, and hug.

"Oh, W-T-F, why do they always do this to me?!" Heidi says. She looks upset and responds in Bengali. Her eyes become teary and she looks at me. "My frickin' parents sent my brothers to take me home for the night. I guess they had it planned all along, but didn't want to tell me 'cuz they knew I'd be pissed off and ruin my game. Seriously, I hate them."

Hamid slaps the back of her head. "Shut up, Hafsa," he says. "Respect the p's. They just wanna keep you safe, you know. Never know what kind of bokachoda are lurking on this campus." I want to tell them that whatever "goat fuckers" are on campus will not touch Heidi as long as I'm near her, but I pretend like I don't know what the word means. Like Heidi and I didn't spend an entire Saturday afternoon looking up Bengali slang on the internet.

I pat her shoulder. "Don't worry 'bout it, Hafsa, you'll be back tomorrow, right?" Her posture has changed, like she's no longer confident or good at anything. She's lost herself.

Fariq answers for her. "Yep. We'll drive her back in the morning. What time is your game?"

"Nine," Heidi says, "So, like, we'll have to leave at seven in the morning. Guess you won't be going out tonight, huh, Fariq. Gotta wake up early and drive me back here just to please baba."

Fariq's eyes are piercing at Heidi and he tells her off in Bengali, stepping away from us, walking until we can barely see him amongst the crowd.

"I'll see you tomorrow, Tirz," Heidi says and hugs me, holding me against her for a while.

I want to tell her that I'll miss her, but instead I blurt, "Yep. Get some rest. One more game, huh?" My jaw gets tight as I bite down on my teeth, pissed at myself for not having the balls to say what I'm feeling.

"It's yours, Tirzah. After tomorrow you'll be ready for the high life!"

"Huh! Let's hope!"

As she walks away, following her brothers, I feel like part of my heart is leaving.

Before dinner, everyone decides to shower in the group dorm-type bathroom. Eight stalls. Thin curtains.

Skye drops her towel revealing the round softness of her backside. It's like a commercial for skincare, promising beauty.

Around us, towels fall. I try not to look but can't help it. There's a round stomach, pillow-shaped, and a dark patch of hair between two thick thighs. Another brown-skinned chest with round perfect breasts and purple nipples. Their bodies disappear behind the showers' curtains, and I'm still in my towel. I walk into my stall, close the curtain. I pull back the curtain and throw my towel toward the bench, making sure if anyone was out there they wouldn't see my naked body.

The water is warm but I'm annoyed at the low water pressure. I need a tough stream of pelting force, not this soft and gentle shower. I run the bar of soap around my body. Around my chest, red and sore, with a small scrape on my right breast where I tried to cut. It seems like a waste. This chest on someone else's body would be almost beautiful, but on me it seems unacceptable. Looking down at my hair, I'm glad it's there to hide what's not there.

My eyes are closed and the water is running down my face when a blast of cold air strikes me. I open my eyes and find Skye holding my curtain back. "Hot-tie!" She shouts, and I'm mortified. Luckily, no one is watching. I grab at the curtain and force it shut. "What the fuck, Skye?" I'm back behind the curtain, unable to see her reaction.

"Tirz, I was just playing around, jeesh! But you never show us what that beautiful body looks like. I mean, you're never there when we shower at school."

I shut the water off. She has ruined my shower. "What if I don't want you to *see* my body? Ever think of that?" I peek my head out. "Grab my towel, will ya, you freak." She's blushing when she hands it to me. Her glance wanders through the small space I've allowed for, and she looks down at my chest.

"Girl, you're gorgeous. You've got, like, the most perfect boobs. Seriously, I'd die to not be the flat girl of the group." She has no idea.

Wrapping the towel around me and tucking in the top corner, tight, so it doesn't fall out, I say, "Maybe some things should just stay private. You know." I scoop up my shampoo.

"I'm just saying I wish I were you. Illinois University drooling all over you. Beautiful chest. Perfect skin. I mean, who wouldn't want to be you?"

"Uh-huh!" I laugh, and answer to myself, Me.

After pizza and a shitload of cherry coke, we're gathered in a common area at the college hotel. There's a TV and some soft plaid couches, and not enough seats for our entire team. I'm sandwiched between Skye and this girl Michelle.

I watch a heavy rain fall outside a window to our left as

the others chit-chat about what to do next. Sol is leaning toward the window's screen, inhaling the earthy rain smells.

Skye whispers something to Michelle who responds, "Noooooo. Really?"

"Let's do it!" Skye shouts and springs up, the couch cushions sink in, sending my body leaning toward Michelle's.

I scoot to the end of the couch cushion so I'm barely even sitting on it.

Skye is bouncing up and down. "Alright. You guys ready for some real fun?"

My heart pumps faster from the cherry coke buzz. "Whatcha got for us, Skye?"

"Rain streaking!" She shouts. And my jaw drops. Yeah. This is my dream come true.

A few teammates say stuff like, "Naw, really?" and "Sounds fun!" and "I'm not doing that!" but most are down with it. Michelle gets up off the couch and claps her hands once. "Alright. This is how I see it. We start off wearing our clothes that we've got on right now. But each time we pass a building, while we're running, we take off something. It's dark. Right? No one should see us."

Skye interrupts, "Yeah. But we gotta stay out of those big lights. Run alongside the buildings by the bushes." She's totally done this before.

"Fo' shiz!" I holler, and have no idea why I'm suddenly gangsta.

"Let's do this thing!" Skye yells, and we all follow like a kindergarten recess line-up.

The rain pelts the ground, but we are protected by the overhang, huddled and second-guessing our plan. But Skye and Michelle give us little time to change our minds. Skye takes off running. Her long legs shining in the rain. We follow in a single-file line, jogging through the wetness. I'm laughing uncontrollably as rain slaps my face. It's hard to see, squinting and jogging.

As we pass a long brick building Skye shouts, "Take it off!" while she pulls her shirt over her head. Still jogging. Her white bra becomes see-through from the rain, and I catch a quick glimpse of hard redness.

Like synchronized swimmers, the rest of the girls pull their shirts off and wrap them around their heads. I do the same, and wrap my t-shirt around my hairline, covering my head.

I am in the middle of our group and turn around to see if the others are topless, too, which, of course, they are. I can't wait to get past the next building. What will they take off next? They could choose their shorts or their bras. One or the other. I'm in my extra small sports bra, so they can't see anything. But if we have to take off our bras, they're gonna see the girl me. Right now, I'm still manlier than they are. They're all in pretty lacy bras with flowers and shit. I'm the only one who's wearing something butchy. But what if Skye chooses her bra over her shorts? Then I'm screwed.

We're coming to the end of a super-tall building in a back alley when Skye yells, "Drop 'em!" And she pulls off her shorts, swinging them around her arm. She yells, "Whoooohoooo!" It's contagious.

Off go the shorts. I gulp. It's like I've been given an early Christmas present, it's wrapped, and, no, I can't open it. But I can look at it and guess what's hiding underneath the wrapping paper. God, I wish I was a guy. But then again, if I was a guy I wouldn't be here. I wouldn't be able to stare at all these beautiful bodies. Instead, I fight the urge to imagine what's hiding underneath Michelle's underwear. What her ass might look like without its cotton covering. What it might feel like to kiss Skye while the rain runs between our half-naked bodies. I fight. The urge.

We're running again: bras and underwear; socks and shoes; wet hair, wet faces, running makeup, slick skin. I'm watching Destiny in front of me: the muscles of her back flexing with her movement. We turn a corner and I'm watching and dreaming, but then my foot slips on a landscaping rock. I fall face-first on the ground. My right knee twists. It burns. I'm hunched over on the ground in pain. The girls from the back of the line stop running. Katie Barnes runs toward me, and I'm not surprised she's the one coming to my rescue. My dad is Christmas card friends with her dad. They went to grad school together, but slowly stopped talking. Just holiday card friends now.

Katie bends over, asking all the right questions, like, if I'm alright, and, what hurts? I assure her that I am fine, and try to get up. My knee is killing me. I can barely walk. I feel like a fool. Injured and half-naked. Wet and upset. If Heidi were here she'd totally help me and take care of me.

I put my clothes back on, fighting the saturated cotton. I think we've lost the group until Skye approaches. "Not again, Tirzah! Lemme help you, poor injured gazelle."

"I'm not a gazelle. At least not an injured one," I joke with Skye.

"I'll take you," she says, covering her pink bra with a wet sweatshirt, and slipping her shorts over her white underwear. "I've got this, Katie, no worries. We'll catch up with ya." Skye wraps her arm around my back and helps me walk. I am so dead. I totally jinxed myself by faking it earlier. Now my knee hurts like a mother.

"Why were you running so much anyway, T? After your injury and all?" Skye asks, holding the door for me to go into the dorms first.

"I'm an idiot," I say, "You know how sometimes things seem worse than they really are, and like, the more you think about them the worse they become?"

"Yeah, totally. I do it all the time—overthink shit."

We're standing alone in the dorm entrance way. "Do you think it's possible to ever go back and fix what's broken?" I ask, getting all philosophical and shit.

"Emerson, dude, you better chill on the pain killers, T!" Skye is laughing at me. "You're overthinking already. I bet you're thinking right now about what I just said about Emerson and overthinking."

"Shut up!" I yell, giggling with her. "Alright. Whatever, but it's true."

Skye motions for us to keep going so she can get me to a couch to sit and rest my knee. "I think you're waaaay overtired and need to stop overanalyzing before I come over and bounce on your knee like Santa's lap."

Skye helps me to the couch, and mocks like she's gonna sit on my knee. She's totally flirting. "You're such a shit!" I say, having no idea that Skye is so freakin' cool. "Such a shit!" I repeat.

"Shit like the stuff that—" I put my hand over her mouth to stop her words.

"As in trouble," I tease. "You're definitely trouble."

11.

The forward from Jefferson High comes charging full-speed at my goal. She looks like a race horse, head bobbing back and forth, her arms pumping with clenched fists. The ball moves ahead with tiny taps of her feet. She is the best forward I've ever played against, and although I've managed the first half of her fierce attempts at a goal, there's a feeling in my gut that this half she'll do anything to get the ball past me. But I'm not gonna let my team down again.

I'm watching her, the sweat from her forehead, her rhythmic running; I think she's gonna shoot at the right corner. I'm ready. I squat down prepared to spring up to block the ball. But then she looks at this tiny girl in the right corner of the field. I'm already in the air, ready to block when the ball's at the feet of the tiny girl. She gives a kick as I'm coming down from my jump. The ball rockets into the right side of the goal. They cheer. I fall to the ground. My right knee pops out all the way to the side as I drop down from my jump. My knee! Fucking rain streaking.

Heidi is at my feet. Her shin guards stain-free from her

little time on the field. "Tirzah, get up! State, Tirzah, we've gotta make it to State." I look up at her face outlined by the sun's glow like a halo. Her arm extends out and I take hold of it. When I'm standing, we hug, and she whispers, "Don't give up, this is your chance. I believe in you." My body fills with warmth, but we let go as the crowd claps. The cheers fuel me and I try to block out the pain in my knee.

By the end of the game, I can barely walk. We've won three to one! We are the regional champions! Queen is blaring from the stadium speakers. We sing. We *are* the champions.

Coach Shoals taps my back. "That's some of the best goal keeping I've ever seen Ms. Maxon. The best. Playing with an injury and all. Wow. I hope this doesn't offend you, but you play just like some of our top guy players. Your coach has done a superb job." Rip brightens up. So do I. He just gave me the best compliment. Yes, I play like a guy. Hell yes.

"No, sir, it's all Maxon, here. She was born with goalie's gloves on."

"So once I file some paperwork with the office, we'll send you the information in the mail. Fill it out as soon as possible so we can get you on our roster. We start in July, so plan ahead now."

"Will do, coach," I say, wiping sweat from my forehead with the sleeves from my jersey. "Thank you for coming to watch. Really. Thank you."

"My pleasure," he says and shakes my hand with a firm squeeze. He clears his throat. "Oh, and do tell your father I said hello."

Back at the dorm hotel Heidi is sad after hearing the story about our rain streaking. "My parents seriously need to let me live. I can't believe I missed a run in the rain. And if I was there I would have caught you as you fell and you might not have fallen. I would have saved you."

"I know," I say and feel guilty that I wasn't thinking about her while running half-naked with the other girls. "I missed you, too." I say, and feel like a jerk.

"I was so lonely last night, Tirz," Heidi says, her eyes have mine locked in some sort of soul-searching glance.

"Me too, Heids. Me, too." I repeat.

On the bus, I'm with Heidi, sitting together. My knee hurts less after three aspirin, or maybe it's just her and the way that I sweat more and hurt less when she's around.

Katie is in the seat diagonal from us. "You're lookin' much better today, T."

"Thanks again for helping me. God that was embarrassing!"

"No prob. Just glad to see you killin' 'em today, even after that fall." She has this sympathetic look on her face that could double as one that warns she has to take a crap.

Heidi nudges me. "Ah-ha. Gettin' close with Katie when I'm not around, huh? So she rescued you?" Heidi puts her fingers up to make quotes for the word rescued. "What's that all about?"

"Shut up!" I nudge back so her body almost slides off our pleather seat. "I fell during the rain streaking bit, but no biggy, I'm fine." I hold my knee. "Well, kind of."

"And Katie, huh?"

"You know she's just a Christmas card friend of the family."

"That's so screwed up. I mean, seriously, they still send you guys Christmas cards and your dads don't even talk."

"Yep." I start giggling. "The funniest thing is that when they first started sending the cards, Mom had no idea who they were. We'd laugh so hard at the letter and picture from a family we didn't even recognize. I think Dad was out of town or something, because I remember him coming home and telling us who they were. But still. Who sends Christmas cards to someone they don't even talk to?"

"That's some weird Christian shit," Heidi says, and her voice bounces as we hit a bump. "Most of the people in my family don't even send cards for Ramadan. Some do. Like, you can send a card after fasting is over, but no one really does."

"You know what I've always wanted to do?"

"No."

"Send random cards to people. Like, maybe we could send random Ramadan cards and sign our names with something fake. Maybe just to our neighbors, and watch them open the cards in their yards. Watch their faces. I bet they'd be all W-T-F and wonder who would send them such a card."

Heidi laughs. "That would be freakin' hilarious. We should do it! But it's not until August. So we have some time."

"K. But we can't forget." I lock pinkies with her, and we

fly our hands together like a butterfly.

"Nothin' like a random Ramadan card to brighten your spirit."

"Happy Ramadan!" I say with a strange accent that sounds more Jersey Jewish than Bengali. Most of the girls around us laugh at my weird outburst. "Sorry. Inside joke," I say to Kate and Luz.

Heidi taps my leg. "OK. For serious now, I gotta tell you something before we get back to school."

A sign out the window says we're sixty miles from Chicago—another ten to our suburb of Oak Park.

"Um, we've got time." I say, pointing the highway sign.

Heidi rests her back against the seat and sits up straight. She leans close. "So, guess what my parents did to me now."

Out the window, I watch a lonely farm. A baby horse chases its mother. "What? I know it was shitty of them to make you go home yesterday, but still. They just wanted you to be safe." Rows of corn outside seem to bend as we speed by.

"No, dude, my freakin' brothers helped my dad figure out how to print my cell phone records. JC's number was on there, like, a ton of times. Dad called JC. I guess we talked for, like, 800 minutes last month and Dad wanted to see who I spent all my time talking to. I have no idea what he said to him, and ohmygod, I've got to face him tomorrow at school. Dad is soooo pissed. I told him we were class partners, but Dad remembered that we had our presentation, like, two weeks ago. I'm so dead."

"Wait. They called JC? Did they, like, talk?"

"Yeah, I think so. I mean, Hamid gave me this huge lecture yesterday the whole way home. That's why Dad sent him to get me. They were worried I'd hang out with JC while we were here."

"Wait, what if they find out about that night with me and the movies? And, Heidi, you've gotta stop with him. He's just so, uh, I don't know. Please. I just don't think he's worth all of this. You know your father could, like, send you back to Bangladesh." I can't look at her. Back out the window, a barn has collapsed from fire or age.

"I said you were dating him and that when we did talk, it was about you."

"What? Why do I always have to take your shit, Heidi?" I meet her eyes; they're almost purple in the sunlight.

"You know they would send me back if they found out I was dating an American guy. A non-Muslim American guy."

"Right. But what about me, Heidi? What about me? What did they say?"

"They don't feel as comfortable about you anymore. Now they're questioning that night I slept over. Wondering if you had guys over. But I totally convinced them that you are nothing but good, and they just told me to watch it. That they're going to watch me closer."

"…" My knee hurts again. "Closer, like how much closer can they watch you?"

"Maybe you shouldn't come over for a couple of weeks. Just until they calm down."

"What?"

"I'm sorry," she says.

But sorry sucks. I grab my duffle bag from the floor and stand up. "That's bullshit, Heidi. Really. Bullshit."

"I'm sure they'll get over it soon. I mean, maybe a week, tops."

"Yeah right."

The bus driver yells, "Hey! Sit down!" I ignore her glare and find an empty seat up front. Screw the fact that the seats were made for two. Everything in this goddamn world is made for two. Hetero hook-ups and marriage proposals. Religious ceremonies and prom dates. Why is everything about finding someone else? Why aren't we alright by ourselves? Why did Heidi have to blame me for that douche JC? I've got to tell her what he did before I lose her forever.

When we arrive at school, I have no energy to give Dad details from the game. It seems like so long ago, and all I can think about is what Heidi just told me—we can't talk for a while.

Dad glances at me from the driver's seat. His hands have a fierce grip of the steering wheel, and I try to break the tension with a half-smile. "You're awfully quiet, kiddo. Everything go alright."

"No, yeah, fine, Dad. I screwed up my knee and played like crap, but I-U is still supposed to send me information. The coach said he's really interested."

Dad runs this whole soliloquy about my knee and how I need to watch it. And I'm trying to find the words to tell him that I don't want to play on the women's team anymore.

"Yeah. But it might not work out, Dad. I totally blew it,

and the coach looked annoyed. They could change their minds, right?"

Dad takes a deep breath and lets it out slowly. "Yeah, they could. Sure. They could change their minds. But honestly, dear, I think one small mistake won't kill your chance on a Division One team. No worries, OK?"

His face changes to bright and cheery. "Just imagine. I could get an adjunct spot there or something. And if you're there—that would be perfect!"

"Perfect, huh?" I remark. Obviously Dad's definition of perfect and my definition come from two totally different worlds.

"Yeparoo!" Dad jokes.

"You're such a dork," I say, and he rubs my head.

I hop out of the car once we pull in the driveway, drop my bags by the opened garage door, and pull my board off the shelf. "Can I go out for a bit, Dad? I just need some time."

He hesitates. "Ah, sure. Just be back before the street lights come on. I'd like to have dinner together at least one night this weekend." Ah. Forgot he was gone at his conference. I've got to ask him how it went. Maybe later.

"Yep, no prob. See you at dinner." I take off down the driveway and cut my board to the left. I don't know where I'm heading, but I want to get there fast. What am I going to do without Heidi? And how long is this gonna last? This is like some bad nightmare. I can't help but think that she could have avoided dragging me into this. I mean, does she want to stop hanging out? Is that why she told her parents that I was the one on the phone with JC? Maybe I was pushing myself on her too much. Maybe she knew how badly I wanted to be with her and she just couldn't take it anymore. Maybe that's why she left Regionals.

I skate faster and faster, pounding my right foot on the ground. Cringing about the pain in my knee. I wish I could talk to her. Wish I could find out more about what she really thought. Tomorrow seems so far away.

What's such bullshit is that I have no interest in guys like JC. I mean, if it was my choice I wouldn't have anything to do with guys like him. But then again, whatever he's doing seems to work with the girls. Like maybe I need to be more of an asshole to get what I want. Or maybe I need a one-inch plastic monkey.

I'm almost to the skate park near school when my knee starts throbbing. There's no way I'm gonna be able to shred like normal. Before anyone can see me wuss out, I head back home.

Dad's in his office, asleep in his chair. I slip down the hallway, grab the opened bottle of wine from the fridge, and slam it. Seriously, something's gotta kill this freakin' tornado in my head telling me to stop playing soccer with girls, to stop looking like a girl, to just be a guy already. Half-buzzed, I grab a pair of scissors from the junk drawer in our kitchen and hide out in my bathroom.

I fucking hate myself for screwing up that game. What was I thinking? If Heidi ever found out it would totally ruin any chance I'd ever have at spending my life with her. I think she totally loves having my heart in her hands. Suck. I'm sick of this shit. This in-between of never really with Heidi, never really one person or another. Never a girl. Never a guy. Never in a relationship. Never the one holding hands in the hallway.

My hands sweat as I cut seven inch clumps of hair from my head, leaving a strip of hair in the center of my head. I grab Hair Pie's buzz clippers, set the guard at one, and begin shaving the sides of my head. I am almost bald all over except the strip of soft-auburn hair down the middle. I want it blue. I want a blue strip of hair down my head. If I'm gonna be an outcast, and the one I love just wants to use me as a cover-up and is never going to want to be my forever, then I'm gonna be that freak on the outside, too.

Someone pounds on the outside of the bathroom door. "What the hell are you doing with my buzzer in there?" Hair Pie yells. I shut it off.

"Nothing. Just, um, shaving a little." He jiggles the door knob and knocks again.

"Open up, Tit-za."

"Go away, Hair Pie!" And then I hear him stomp down the hall to Dad's office.

"You better come, Dad, she won't open the door," and blah-blah-blah. I hear his whiney voice, but block it back out with the buzzer, and clean up the back of my hair so you can only see little specs of brown on my scalp.

The door flies open and Dad rubs his thin arm. He gasps. "Whaaat? Whaat happened? What did you do? Tirzah. What in the world were you thinking?" He looks down at the pile of hair at my feet. He puts his hand on my scalp and quickly pulls away. "My god you look like a skinhead. Is that what this is all about? Are you trying to make a political statement here? What is this?"

"Wait, no. It's nothing political. Just wanting a change. That's all. Just something different. I'm sick of looking like everyone else." I check myself in the mirror. I'm pale and sickly with shaven hair. The patch on top makes me look really hardcore. "This is just something different. No worries, Dad."

Hair Pie snatches the buzzer from my hands. "Don't even think about saying we're related anymore. Got it?"

"Are you serious right now? You're gonna act like you don't know me just because I shaved my head?"

"It's a frickin' landing strip. Your head looks like a big blue muff!" Hair Pie slides past Dad and out of sight. I flick him off.

"Alright now. That's enough!" Dad pauses and takes a deep breath. "As long as everything's alright as you say it is. I can accept this new look of yours, but I don't wanna be there when your mother sees it."

"You wouldn't be there anyway. Right? Like when's the last time you two were in the same room anyway?" Now I'm sarcastic and feel like an asshole. I've just morphed myself and smarted off to my dad. He turns his back to me. After his footsteps fade, I hear his office door slam. I've screwed up. Totally.

12.

In home ec class, Mrs. K. talks about couples' massages, suggesting that once we get married, it's good to have non-sexual contact with your partner. I wonder when they're gonna rewrite the textbook and add a chapter on same-sex marriages. It's bad enough that we have to carry around an egg and pretend like it's our child for three weeks, but then they make us "marry" someone in our class. And now Mrs. K. wants to teach me how to please my partner without being sexual. Yeah right.

JC's behind me. Actually, he's always behind me in home ec, but today it bothers me. His heavy cologne chokes me. Then I see his hand with a piece of paper folded into an origami bird.

I open the note, wondering if there's some sort of apology or something for the party incident. Or maybe a letter about Heidi and how he knows how much I love her, and he finally wants to tell me he's giving up on her.

I pull at the bird's paper head and open its wing. As it loses shape, a drawing appears on the page: a picture of a hand rubbing someone's privates. A cartoon bubble above the picture says, "Ooo, baby! Massage my man parts! Oh yeah, right there!" I cringe and crumple the paper, shoving it in my folder when Mrs. K. walks up to my desk and puts her hand out. I go ten shades of red.

"Ms. Maxon? Is there something you want to share with the class?"

"Um. Really interesting lecture, Mrs. K. That's all. Thank you." I put my head down so the blue flap of hair covers my eyes. Mrs. K's red-nailed hand reaches inside my folder. She unwraps the crumpled paper. My cheeks get hot and my throat dries. I swallow hard.

"Well, I can see that you all got absolutely nothing out of that lecture. Is that so? Who drew this tasteless picture?" She bends down so we're eye-level. "Huh, Ms. Maxon? Who drew this? You?"

"God no. It was just passed to me." I wish I said JC's name. Maybe ratting him out would get him in trouble and away from me for a few days.

She paces in front of the smart board. "One last time, Ms. Maxon. Who passed this note to you?" She stops moving as if waiting for some epiphany on my part.

I sit up straight. My butt tingles as I move, numb from my slouched spot on my chair. I could take this moment to bust JC, possibly get him a week's worth of detentions. Then he wouldn't be able to walk Heidi to her car every day and kiss by the door.

"I did it," I say, my hand over my mouth like I don't want to be seen admitting to some pervert's artwork. But then again, Heidi would want me to cover for JC. Dad's gonna kill me if I get a detention. Rip will flip, too. That'd mean I'd be late to practice. Shit. Shit. Shit.

Mrs. K. takes another look at the picture. She shudders. "Alright, Ms. Maxon, in the hall."

Covering for JC got me five days of after-school detention, and as I was cursing myself for being such a douche and taking his heat, he stops me in the hall. No joke.

The blue slip sits on top of my books like some scarlet letter.

JC says, "You saved my ass. I owe you one, totally." I'm taken back by his friendliness, and accept his thanks. After all, I was the one who was sentenced for taking his slack.

"It was nothing," I tell him when really it's everything. I mean, I should have gotten him in trouble. But why? So he'd hate me even more? Five afternoons didn't seem that bad anyway.

I'm almost at my pre-calc class when JC says, "Wait. I'm having a little get-together at my place on Saturday. My mom's having some Tupperware thing and said I could have a few friends over. Kinda lame, but you can come if you want." I'm in shock. The class prick is inviting me to his house and I actually want to go.

"Sure. Yeah. Rad. What time?"

"I dunno. Eight, maybe."

I'm about to walk into class when he says, "Hey. Bring Heidi, too. K?"

"Yep. I mean, I'll see if she can make it. I don't know with her parents and all, but I'll check."

"Yeah. Her dad and I talked for, like, an hour one night. He wanted to know my intentions with his daughter. I tried to sound cool and all, telling him about our class project and school work, but after that he wouldn't let her talk to me on the phone again—"

"I know. Believe me. I know. But at least you still get to be with her at school."

"Yeah. Whatever. Anyway, just bring her, too, alright?"

"Cool." We bump knuckles and I slip into class, late. Mr. Terpinas squints his eyes at me as I walk in the door, and scribbles something in his attendance book. Great, I'm tardy. JC is ruining my day.

At my locker, Heidi skips toward me. She stares at my hair. Her eyes appear to tear up and she shakes her head. I'm all nervous wondering what she's really thinking. From her face, she hates it.

I want to tell her I miss her. She's in that fuzzy velour hoodie, the grey one that makes her look like a wide-eyed stuffed animal. I want to hug her. I smile, nervous.

"Kind of weird, huh? I just got sick of the long stuff." I run my fingers through what's left of my hair, the small strip on the top.

She looks down at the bottom of her locker. "Um, yeah. Well, you've certainly gotten rid of most of it. And, um…" She stands up so our eyes meet. "What the hell were you thinking, Tirzah? I mean, seriously, my father is never gonna let you in my house looking like that. Look at you. You look like a dude."

"Ya think?"

"Why are you smirking? You want to look that way? Are you serious? That's what your goal is or something?"

"No. I mean, I don't know. It's just something different, ya know. I kinda like it. But your dad, I thought he was mad at me."

"I spent the night convincing him that you're a good friend, and not trouble, and that time I slept at your house was totally innocent. I told him you were just taking care of a sleepy me." She looks sad. "But now, with that freak wig, I don't know what he's gonna think."

I can't believe she spent the weekend trying to make me look good when I was in self-destruct mode. I'm such an asshole.

"I'll wear a hat. I mean, if you think he'll really let me hang out with you again, I'll cover this up."

Skye bumps Heidi's hip. "Hey, girls. Ready for Trig?" Uh. I get this sick feeling my stomach. My hands are clammy. Why do I get so uncomfortable when Skye and Heidi are together?

Skye runs her fingers through my strip of hair. "Sweet new do, T. You look kinda hardcore, Skater."

I turn my head to the side to get the hair off my face. "Something different, ya know. I got kinda sick of hiding behind all that hair." I say the words slow, hoping Heidi will jump back in the convo.

But she's totally oblivious, flipping through a folder for something. "I'll catch ya later." Heidi says.

"Wait," I call out. "JC wants us to come over Saturday night."

Heidi freezes. "Both of us. Like me and you?"

"Yep, I totally covered for him and took the heat for some crap-ass note he was passing around. Mrs. K. gave me a detention. Now we're B-F-Fs or something."

Heidi looks thrilled. "Awesome! Sure. Yeah. We'll have to figure out something to tell the po-po. But yeah. I'm in, for sure!"

"Totally tubular!" I joke, mocking her overly happy tone.

"You're such a bitch," she says. "But I still love ya!" An air kiss leaves her hand.

"Love you, too, bitch."

Skye nudges me. "Feelin' a little left out of the lovefest here."

I nudge her back. "Love you too, biotch."

She smirks. "I can tell."

At five minutes to seven, Mr. Chaudhary pulls onto my driveway. He gets out and waits for Heidi. She opens the car door, looking smokin' hot in jeans and a t-shirt.

Mr. C. waves to me as I stand in the doorway. "Hello, dear," he says. "I'll be back at ten-thirty. This way we don't have to worry about my little sleeping beauty." I'm so happy he's not mad, I could just squeeze his chubby cheeks.

"Yep. Thanks, Mr. C. We'll see you in a little bit." I lean on the front door, my palms sweaty as I wonder if he's gonna ask me what we're doing. "Sure you don't want me to drive her home. It's not a problem or anything."

He opens the driver's side door of his nineties sedan. "No worries. I'll be back. But thank you anyway. You two have

95

fun doing your girls' thing." He ducks his head into his car. I watch him pull away as Heidi walks up the drive with a face like a winning contestant on the Hellz Yeah I Lied to My P's Again show.

She throws up a high-five. "Ready for our at-home spa night?"

"I'm ready to be facialized," I joke. "Wait. Or whatever you say when you're getting a facial." She giggles. I give her a low knuckle knock, and wonder if she'd have spent an hour convincing her dad that we're going to have a spa night if it wasn't for JC's get-together. I mean, would she even want to hang out if it wasn't for JC?

"You are made of amazing things, T. Seriously, when I die they better erect a statue of you and put it by my grave that says 'Queen of Awesome.'"

"Person of Awesome," I say as we head up the stairs to my room. "I'm no queen. And, yes, you owe me one…again! Why am I always blocking your shit, lady? Always. When are you gonna block me?" I mock a goalie's chest bump against the wall, smashing my chest.

"Just ask," she says, while picking at something on her face in the mirror. "I'd have your back; you just never have any drama." She backs away from the mirror and holds my arms. "T, that hair. Um, you look like a goy."

"A what?"

"A goy. Half girl. Half boy."

I break out of her arm hold. "Whatevah. Psssht! If I'm a goy then you my biotch." I throw my shoulders back, bobbing and weaving my body like some bad ass boxer. "Fo shnizle double dizzle."

"Fo' shniz. I'll be your biotch." She tickles my waist. It makes me blush.

"For real. We better go. You only have, like, two hours until we have to get back here for your pops."

We race each other down the stairs and I holler to Dad that I'll be home in a couple of hours. He shouts "alright" from his office, and peeks his head around the corner, still on his wheely chair.

"Nice to see you, Heidi!" he calls out.

JC's condo smells like bacon when we walk through the door. There's a group of women huddled around two floral couches and some chairs with a lady in the center talking with a really high-pitched voice. Almost fake-sounding, or too theatrical for a Tupperware salesperson.

"Hi, girls!" A woman waves from the middle of the couch, and I assume it's JC's mom.

Heidi and I wave back as JC comes up the stairs and stands in the hallway. "Hey. We're all down here," he says, and then waits for us to follow him.

I glance back at the Tupperware group, at the salesperson: her wide body, and red-knuckled hands. For some reason, I get this feeling she's a guy.

JC, Ty, Derek, and his girlfriend, Celeste, are huddled around the TV playing Madden. Gag me. They're cheering and swearing while I sit on an old couch and watch like some video game spectator. On the floor, JC puts his hand in Heidi's lap, and she locks fingers with him. Double-gag me.

Why did I say I'd come here again?

After twenty minutes of watching cartoon figures in tight pants play football, and Heidi cuddle with JC, I try to remind myself that there is nothing between Heidi and me. That the love I feel for her can never be more than friendship because she isn't gay or doesn't like me that way or whatever. That her bi-curiousness means nothing when badass JC's around. But it's kinda like a quick trip to hell where I know I'm going to be allowed back in heaven, but for the moment the devil has decided to torture my ass by twisting my heart into little knots.

Ty takes a seat by me. "Dude, you wanna go upstairs and grab some munchies? Mrs. G. made these bacon things that are killer."

"Yep. I'll go up, as long as we don't have to hang out with the Tupperware club."

"They won't even notice. Come on." I follow Ty up the stairs.

We tiptoe on the linoleum floor. There's a platter of quiche, quesadillas, and things wrapped in bacon, and next to that, several bowls of dips and chips. Ty loads up a paper plate, while I follow. We're pouring some Coke into cups when the Tupperware person makes her way into the kitchen. She's totally staring at me and my hair.

"Uh, hi, I'm Tirzah," I say, and look down to avoid her stares. And that's when I see her feet. Size twelve, at least! But almost bigger, like dad's feet smashed into black sandals.

"Aunt Bev," she says, and scoops some spinach dip from a bread bowl with her masculine hands. There is a small amount of stubble peeking out from underneath the cuff of her blouse. "You're a friend of JC's, right? He's told me about you. Soccer champ, right?"

"I guess. Yep." I look at Ty to add to the convo, but he's already inching toward the stairs. Aunt Bev goes on and on about playing soccer in high school, too, and how it was the best thing for her. But she was a forward and not a goalie, and oh my god, you should have seen how good Mellor was back then, and she's still heard they are good now. I tell her they are still one of the best and finish pouring my drink. I'm about to say something like 'nice meeting you' to this Aunt Bev person when she says, "Come help me put some stuff in my car, won't you?" She points to the dining room where boxes are stacked high. OK. So we're, like, tight now all the sudden, and I'm her little Tupperware elf, carrying shit for her so she can deliver more plastic bowls to good boys and girls who made it on the nice list.

I follow her to the table and lift a few boxes. We head through the garage and out on the driveway. She opens the door to her red mini hybrid.

"Yeah, JC's mentioned you. You know, I was like you, too, in high school."

I set the boxes into her trunk. "Like me? Right. Soccer again, huh? I skateboard, too. Probably better at soccer, though."

She stops moving and pats at something under her eye.

Her silence makes me nervous. "Wait, what do you mean?"

Her voice is lower now. "I transitioned after my divorce.

Used to be Ben. Now I'm Beverly."

"Really? Is it that obvious? I mean, how could you tell that I'm that way?" I ask, but silently applaud myself for noticing her gender bend from the get-go.

"You always know your own kind, honey. But for me it took years of therapy and hormone replacement, and finally I was ready for the transition. I spent many years denying it. Even married a friend from high school thinking some hetero marriage would magically erase the fact that I was transgender." She shifts some boxes and bowls in her trunk before closing the hatch.

"So that didn't go so well, huh?" I ask.

"Ha! Nope. But no hard feelings, thank God. And no kids, either."

I want to hug her for some reason. Like maybe it's the fact that no one's ever really talked to me like her. No one's ever understood what was going on in my head and body.

And then I just open up. "But wait. I thought I was just gay. You know, into girls. And maybe there's some other stuff I'm dealing with in my head, but you're talking about something that I'm not sure I am. I mean, how did you know you were trans?"

She tugs at her nylons. "There was this book called *True Selves*. Changed. My. Life. I knew I wasn't alone. You know. I just knew that was me."

She motions for us to go back inside when I say, "Oh yeah. Well maybe I'll check it out, but I barely have time for anything else besides soccer and school and more soccer."

"I'm just sayin'. It'll help. A lot." She leads me back into the kitchen as another mom-type wanders in a grabs a paper plate. I want to ask Aunt Bev to talk more, but I know she's working and all.

"Hey, if you ever need any Tupperware as a gift for your parents, just send me an e-mail or give me a call." She scribbles something, hands me her card, and winks. The words "True Selves" are written on the back.

"Yeah, thank you. I'm sure my mom would be much happier with colorful plastic storage thingies. Or my dad. Or whoever." I'm stumbling because all I want to say is thank you Fairy Godmother. I look for a wand in her poufy costume skirt; there isn't one. But there is an e-mail address on the business card—bitchsellsbowls@yahoo.com.

My heart is beating fast as I head down the stairs. I feel like the world finally gets me. Like maybe there are a whole group of people that feel the way I do. Trapped inside the wrong body. But then my happy buzz is killed when Heidi and JC aren't sitting with the group. Please tell me they're not off making out somewhere.

After twenty minutes of no sign of Heidi and JC, I decide to go find them. I knock on the bedroom door and feel like an ass. I mean, I know Heidi's all grown up and shit and I should probably just let her be, but that's Heidi. My Heidi.

I lean against the door. "It's ten, and we'd better go so we're there before your dad." I'm talking to a leftover piece of tape on the grainy wood. JC probably ripped down his Justin Bieber poster right before we came over so we wouldn't make fun of him.

JC clears his throat, and I hear giggling. "Yep. I'll be right out. OK?" More giggling. I want to open the door, just a crack, to see what he's doing to her. Or what she's doing to him. And then Aunt Bev calls my name.

I meet her halfway up the stairs. She's hunched over in an awkward position from the low ceiling. "Hey, I just thought of something. Before I go, there's this panel at the College of DuPage about being TG. Kinda cool, you know, where TG men and women talk about their journeys. You should go, if you can make it." I'm glad she's whispering. Wouldn't want anyone downstairs to hear.

"Yeah. No, that sounds cool. I'll try and make it."

Aunt Bev shakes her head. "Good. I think it's Tuesday night at seven. But I'll check, and when you e-mail me, I'll find out for sure before getting back to you."

"Awesome. Thanks, um, Bev."

"Aunt Bev," she says. "K. Have fun down there." She peeks a little farther down the stairs, looking around the wall. "JC, where are you? I'm leaving. Come give me a smooch!"

JC's door handle rattles. "Right here, Aunt Bev." His hair's all screwed up. I want to barf.

JC approaches and climbs a few stairs. He hugs his aunt. "Good to see you," he says.

"You be careful, mister," Bev scolds. "Teenage pregnancy is on the rise, along with warts and nasty things like that." Bev crinkles her large nose.

JC turns red. "It's not like that at all."

"Mm-hmmm. Sure," Bev says, and grabs JC's chin. "Can't hide from the truth, you know. Can never hide from the truth." God I love her. Seriously.

And once Aunt Bev walks back up the stairs, Heidi sneaks out of JC's room. When she sees me her face looks panicked. "You ready to go. I mean, maybe if we go now, we'll even have time to paint our nails or something, so my dad will think we were spa-nighting."

I'm getting kind of sick of being the cover-up. I don't answer her, and instead just head up the stairs, say my goodbyes, and wait for her in the car.

After a silent ride home, we pull down Iroquois Trail. Mr. Chaudhary's car is in the driveway, but he's not in it.

"Oh, fuck. Where's my dad?" Heidi rolls down the window. "I think I'm gonna hyperventilate." Her breathing is heavy and panicked—in and out, out and in.

"Stop. It'll be fine. We'll just, I don't know, think fast. Where were we?" I take my foot off the gas so we're going, like, two miles per hour, inching closer to my driveway.

"Um. Oooooh. I don't know." Heidi makes this scary wind sound through her teeth. "K. Got it. Let's just say we were at Skye's house watching the video from Regionals."

"Oh. Good one. Yeah, that'll work," I say sarcastically.

In the house, Mr. Chaudhary is leaning back in the Lazy Boy recliner, a cup of tea in hand. Dad is on the couch, legs crossed, hands moving. They're talking about London; Dad's telling his traditional story about riding on the moped in the middle of the night past a guy shot on the corner. He's still traumatized. The conversation stops when we are

103

standing within a few feet from our dads.

Mr. Chaudhary stands. "Ah, there they are. And how was your *spa night*, my dears?" His eyes are bulging.

Heidi crosses one leg over the other and clasps her hands together. "Oh. Change of plans. We went to Skye's to watch Regionals."

"Change of plans," Mr. C. mocks. "And you couldn't have called me to inform me of this change?"

They continue bickering over rules until Mr. C. stops talking, mid-sentence. He looks at my head, and I'm freaking because I hadn't put my hat back on. Didn't think he'd be in my living room when we got home. My hats are in my bedroom, but now there's no time to cover up.

He stands up and comes closer to me. "Tirzah, your hair," he looks back at my father, "my goodness, is this a new style or something?"

My father wipes his forehead with his hand. "Ugh. I don't know. Teenagers, you know? I can't seem to keep up with the modern styles, and Tirzah here said she was ready for a change. I, um," he takes a deep breath, "have decided to view it as a matter of personal expression."

"Well—" Heidi's dad interrupts. "In my culture women do not shave their heads. Long hair is part of a woman's beauty." He motions toward Heidi's long hair.

"Understandable. Very understandable," Dad says, seemingly embarrassed.

Heidi gently holds her father's hand and addresses him in Bengali. He whispers something, sounding aggravated, then turns to the both of us and says, "We'd better get going.

Her mother will worry. Thank you for the tea and biscuits." He extends his hand to my dad, who is now standing with us. They shake and say goodbye.

Heidi whispers, "I can't believe we let him see your hair. I'm never gonna hear the end of this." She stops and pulls me farther from our fathers so we're in the hallway by the door. "He told me to find a new friend."

I lean close and whisper back, "Seriously?"

"Yeah. That's what he just told me, so basically we're so screwed."

Mr. Chaudhary approaches, looking at me like he's disappointed. Like I'm no longer his favorite Blakean girl. He forces a smile, takes Heidi's hand in his, and heads for the door.

After they leave, Dad gives me a small lecture about telling the truth, but it doesn't last long, and it ends with him telling me that he's proud that I wasn't drinking and was home by 10:15. I'm pretty lucky.

In my room, I put my iPod on and try to bury myself in my favorite songs. But all I can think of is Heidi, and that I probably won't be allowed at her house again. And why do her parents have to judge me because of my shaved head? Like that means I'm a bad person. I understand culture and religion and everything, but isn't religion based on love? No matter what you believe in, most religions just offer some sort of road map for people to follow so, like, they don't go crazy or something. Seriously. I get that Heidi's Muslim, but Muslims base their religion on love and respect, patience and guidance. And even though I might not look the way other girls should, I'm still a good person. Even if my outsides shout hardcore goy, my insides just want someone to love and someone to love me back.

When Dad's asleep, I sneak out my bedroom window, down the wooden deck to meet Skye at some random party at Ty's that she texted me about.

When I walk in, everyone's congratulating me on Illinois University's interest, pouring Jell-O shots down my throat. Next thing I know, I can't see straight, and then I'm at a table where Ty and some guys are playing quarters with shots of whiskey.

After missing the shot glass with my quarter three times, and nearly choking on whiskey, all I wanna do is make-out with someone. My body is tingly and warm and ready for another warm and tingly somebody. My God, it's been a while since Skye and I made out after we watched some late-night movie on Cinemax.

On Skye's tenth glance my way, I get up from Ty's vinyl kitchen chair and make my way across the room. It spins in a nice clockwise motion, like we're on a slower version of the tilt-a-whirl where you can walk from one side to the other and pick someone to make-out with. I'm in front of Skye and there isn't anything said between the two of us before she says, "Thought you'd never ask." She heads for the stairs, looks around to see if anyone notices, and then whispers in my ear, "Meet me in the guest bedroom in three minutes."

"Mmm-hmm," I say in her ear.

I have three minutes to think about what's gonna happen between me and Skye. I mean, I know she totally digs me, but as a chick and not anything else. But I want her to dig me more like a guy. I want her to let me be a guy, but I've got nothing for her. I rinse my hands in the sink and take a long look at my face. I run my fingers along my square jawline. I splash a little water from the faucet on my face to wake my ass up so I'm ready for whatever Skye needed three minutes to prepare for. Or maybe she just didn't want people seeing us walking upstairs together.

The upstairs hallway is dark and the guest room door is closed, but I've been in there so many times in junior high when we used to play Seven Minutes in Heaven, and I'd spend seven minutes trying to fight off whichever guy I got. Bad memories, all of them, except the one time I felt Chad Olsen's penis through his pants. Didn't get anything from touching it, but felt the outline of it, trying to imagine would be like to have something like that between my legs—a tiny arm with a brain of its own.

Skye's under the covers. My heart beats fast. I hiccup and taste the whiskey, and fight the urge to throw up.

"There you are," she says. Her voice is all flirty and soft. Her clothes are in a pile on the floor, so I take off my pants, leaving on my sports bra, loose guys' boxers, and a t-shirt. Skye is wearing a sheer white thong with a pink ruffle around the top. Her breasts are perfectly round, her stomach soft and pale. My God, she's gorgeous with thick thighs. I close my eyes, but open them quickly when my head spins in circles.

She lays her head above my chest and runs her fingers along my chin. Then my ear. Then back to my mouth. Her fingertip is soft against my lips and I open my mouth. Kiss her finger. And then it's inside my mouth. I'm sucking on it. She moves her body against mine. I close my eyes and we kiss and she moves on top of me. We grind on each other with so much passion that I feel like I'm gonna explode. All I want to do is be in her, somehow, but instead I just touch her and watch her face which tells me how much she enjoys what I'm doing.

We stop for a while and she puts her head near my neck, her body close to my side. She rubs my arms, then my legs. "You've got the best body. All these tight muscles." And she kisses my arm.

"And you've got this body that, um, my God, it's just so amazing." She stops kissing and lies next to me so we are eye-level and gives me that look. She's smiling and her eyes won't leave my glance.

Then she rolls off the bed. "This was nice. Really, really nice."

"Yeah. Uh-huh. Nice." Nice like what? Nice like that's the last time we're gonna do anything, or nice like pretty please I want another turn.

Once we're dressed and on the stairs, heading back down toward the rest of the crowd, she says really loud-like, "So, can you believe that? I mean, thanks for listening and all, Tirzah. You're such a good friend." She hugs me at the bottom of the stairs, and there are, like, eight people that have witnessed her performance. I should have known that "nice" meant never tell anyone.

I swallow whatever ounce of confidence I just had in the bedroom and head out the front door.

13.

The following Tuesday, I'm psyched to meet Aunt Bev at the TG panel. When I get to the college, Aunt Bev is waiting in a purple overcoat just beyond the entrance doors.

"Hello, daaaahling," she draws her words, waving her hand elegantly. I say hello and listen as my words echo in the corridor.

A sign behind her reads: "Transitions: A Panel for Members of the Transgender Community and its Allies."

"Allies?" I ask Aunt Bev. She motions for us to start walking toward the auditorium.

"Our friends, basically. There are plenty of people out there who support us, but they aren't necessarily trans. But we need them, ya know, for backup. The louder our voices the more informed people will be. More info equals less hate."

"That's awesome," I say. "We've got something like that at school, but it's more LGB, no T, though."

"We're getting there," she says, while we find a seat in the fifth row of the auditorium.

There are five people seated at a long, wooden table, with mics on stands and pitchers of water. Totally official. I almost feel underdressed in jeans and a t-shirt.

What's weird is that I can't tell the people are trans. And maybe they aren't, but I thought that's what the panel was all about. The guys look like dudes and the women, well, yeah, they look just like women.

A blonde woman clears her throat and speaks into the microphone, welcoming us, introducing the panel and the topic: Transgender Athletes. That's why Bev wanted me to come. I nudge her. "Thank you, Fairy Godmother."

She winks a false eyelash and fakes an air kiss.

Talk in the crowd fades. I scan the audience to see if I know anyone. Like maybe someone I go to school with is secretly trans, too. But really we're kinda far from home, and that'd be a long shot.

The blonde lady asks the first question, something totally basic. "What's the pulse of the sports world with regard to transgender athletes?"

I want to raise my hand and answer part of the question because I wanna talk about that TG woman on the girls' basketball team. But someone beats me to it: a spokesperson for the NCAA. No shit, the NCAA is here?

The College Athletic Association rep spews out a hell of a lot of information about new rules about transgender athletes. And basically, TG guys can play on a guys' team, but TG women play on co-ed teams. Or something like that. I really don't focus on much but the part that includes me. I can play on a guys' team.

Some Big Ten rep steps in and adds that each college has different rules, and like some TG recruit, says, "We now have a medical technician that deals strictly with our transgender athletes."

Bev taps my lap. "Hear that, kid? You might not have to wait."

After listening to the panelists, I don't want to leave. It's like I'm Dorothy and I've made my way to Oz with Glinda the Good Witch, and even though there's no place like home, this place feels better than anywhere.

But the question is: Where do I go from here?

14.

Heidi sends a text on Monday morning, six minutes before I have to walk out the door.

"Don't pick me up. Hamid's takin' me. Suck! TTYL"

I stare at my phone and wonder what I'm supposed to type back, and maybe I shouldn't because her father's probably still monitoring her phone. I send back a quick "K," and head out to my car. Maybe we'll have a few minutes to talk before class.

Heidi's already waiting at my locker. "Front door service isn't so bad. I even beat you here." Her face looks sad, her eyes sunken a little lower.

"Shut up. You look miserable." I sift through my locker for my books.

"It's like I'm on lockdown. They're checking my e-mails, texts, phone calls. Dad says I betrayed him by lying about where we were going. Good thing he really believes that we went to Skye's. But you know what, I totally wish he knew we went to JC's because nothing happened. Yes, we messed around, but I wouldn't sleep with him, or let him sleep with me, and I think that's what Dad thinks all guys want. I don't know. Now my brothers have to take me to school. I can't use my e-mail or phone. I'm seriously in jail right now."

"Are you serious? They're watching you that close?" The hallway gets louder. People are tapping us on our backs and saying hi, but I can't look at anyone because my best friend is falling apart in front of me.

Her eyes get teary. "They won't let me go out anymore. And soccer. One of my brothers is gonna be at practice. Watching."

"That sucks. But we only have one more meet before soccer's over. This isn't fair. I mean, how can they do this to you? You're seventeen. What about your job? Are they gonna make you quit that, too?"

"Oh, right. Yeah, I can still work and deposit money in the family account. Even that is starting to piss me off because I don't even have my own bank account. Why does all my money have to go to my family?" The bell rings to warn of five minutes before first period begins.

"Alright. Just take one day at a time. You're gonna get through this, and maybe they'll start to give you a little more freedom each day. Ya never know." I hug her, feeling her sweaty forehead against my neck. It's like she's melting and there's nothing I can do.

"Baba wants to go home." Heidi's warm tear hits my neck and runs down to my shoulder.

"Go home like where?"

"Back home. He's going for an interview, but thinks he'll

be hired as a professor in Dhaka."

There's nothing for me to say. Sometimes some things just aren't worth fighting anymore. "If baba thinks you should go, there's nothing I can do to keep you here." It's like my stomach ate tiny holes in my heart.

All I can say is, "I'm here for you. We can still hang out at lunch. Right? Can talk over corndogs and fried fingers. Maybe he won't get the job, or maybe the museum will give him a raise. You never know, right?"

She laughs. "You know him. When his mind's set on something, that's it." She straightens up. "But you're right. There are always fried fingers." That's what we call the chicken strips that look more like body parts and really have no meat in them. Just scrumptious fried stuff.

"Ever notice the lunch lady is missing her pinky?" I ask, doing anything to get Heidi to laugh.

It works, and we're giggling our way down the hall. Heidi bends her pinky so it's hidden. She pretends to scoop up some imaginary food, and holds out her hand with the missing finger. "Chicken, girls? Today's special. Four fingers—uh, I mean, four pieces for a dollar." We laugh our way to the lunchroom.

The cafeteria is pure energy: voices and laughter, shrieks and whispers—a morning's worth of trapped personality waiting to exhale from the insides of high school regurgitation. We spend all morning listening to lectures and doing state-mandated lessons, dying to freakin' express ourselves. If I knew how, I'd play a guitar or something right in the middle of the sunken down part of the caf where the stoners hang. We'd sing songs from the Beatles about blackbirds and holding hands.

Heidi and I find Skye and the group gathered around Sludge who is gazing down the nose of a milk carton. "What the frick, JC, how am I supposed to drink this shit?!"

JC, Ty, and the group are laughing their asses off.

Ty clears his throat and widens his eyes. "How you could NOT eat when there are starving children all over the world is beyond me. Waste not want not," he sings like some high-pitched school teacher.

Sludge looks in the carton again as I find a spot next to Ty, trying to avoid eye contact with Skye.

JC slaps me five and gives me a what-up. I what-up him back and shiver from the weirdness that exists between us, wondering if his aunt told him about our talk.

"What's he got?" I ask out loud.

"Oh, ya know, a little pizza dipping sauce, some pepper, Ty's root beer, veggie medley, ketchup, one lonely chicken finger, and, oh yeah, whatever chocolate milk was left in there," JC says.

"Niiice," I answer.

"Alright douchebags. This one's for the hungry kids in the province of Islamabadustan." Sludge lifts the carton.

"If you're gonna drink for someone, at least drink for something for real," Skye adds.

Sludge pushes her comment off with the wave of his hand and chugs. His cheeks turn red as his Adam's apple moves up and down while he swallows. He stops and holds the carton far away from himself. Then he lets out a ridonkulously long burp that smells like sour milk and garlic.

"OOOoooooh, ssssssick!" Skye hollers. "You're next, Tirzah!" She jokes. I'm sweaty, though, wondering what else she might say.

"Never!" I shout back while Sludge cringes and swallows something in his throat. I watch his Adam's apple move down his neck like a small mouse trapped on a miniature slide under his skin. Or maybe it looks more like an apple than a mouse. And the whole mouse in the neck image freaks me out. Either way, will I ever get one of those? I look around at the table. All the guys have variations of produce hanging from their necks. I might need an apple instead of this smooth, straight skin. Is that even possible?

My stomach turns and I need fresh air. "Heids, come outside with me real quick," I say, and she doesn't even hesitate. She's right there with me.

I squint from the sun's super-brightness, in pain from the adjustment between inside and outside lighting.

"You and JC seem all buddy-buddy," Heidi says, picking the outside off a fried finger. She hands it to me.

Munching on the breading, I answer, "I know, right, he was acting like my new BFF."

"Kinda weird, no?"

"Yeah. I thought so, too. But maybe he's just feeling guilty about getting me in trouble. I still have that damn detention after school today. Seriously the last thing I wanna do."

Heidi finishes chewing. "Hey, I tried to call you last night, but didn't hear back. Did your dad tell you?"

"You called my house? For real, dork? I kept trying to get a hold of you, but you dropped off the face of the earth."

"I actually couldn't remember your cell number. You're in my contacts in my now-held-hostage cell phone, but seriously, I couldn't remember it. 640-129-something. Or 2-1, or I don't know. But I know your home phone by heart from when we were little."

"Funny. No, yeah, I wasn't home. I was at this—uh—meeting thing with, uh, JC's aunt." My armpits are sweaty and I wonder if rings are starting to bleed through my cotton long-sleeved t-shirt.

"Bev? What, are you going to sell Tupperware now or something?"

I laugh. "No. God no. But we met at C-O-D for a panel on transgender athletes."

Heidi freezes. "Transgender like Chas Bono?"

"Yep. I mean he wasn't there, but yeah, people like him. Like Aunt Bev."

And then we get into this whole convo on how Heidi swears Aunt Bev is a woman, like she wants to have a thumb war and all, and she'd even bet me her entire wardrobe on the fact that Aunt Bev is a she. But of course I know I'll win and then she'd have nothing to wear ever, so I refuse to make the bet on something that I already know is true.

I turn on my cell phone to check the time. "Crap! We've only got two minutes."

"Whatever. Just keep going," Heidi coaxes.

"K. Well there was this athletic rep there from the NCAA who said it's alright for TG men to play on men's teams, and it got me thinking, why can't I play on a men's team?"

Heidi stands up. Well, she kinda jumps up and grabs my shoulders. "Seriously?! You think it's alright to just all the sudden be a guy and play on a guy's team when you, like, always played as a girl. Like that's not going to be weird or anything?"

My mouth drops and I stop liking life all of the sudden. That's not the response I wanted.

"Maybe. I mean, I don't know. I'm trying to figure it all out. First I've gotta figure out if that's really me, and I'm still in this in-between where I don't know if that's really me, so I'm supposed to see some doctor Bev recommends. But you think it'll be that weird?"

Heidi looks sad. "I just wonder what people will think." She pauses and does that long eye stare thing that makes me nervous.

"That's what this is all about? What people think? Not what I think or I want, but what people think. What about JC? Have you ever wondered what people think about him and you? He's only the biggest manwhore around."

"Take it back," Heidi demands, "Take that back."

But the words have already left my mouth, and I can't get them back.

"What's that supposed to mean, anyway? JC's not a manwhore."

I have a moment where the truth battles around in my head. If I tell her the truth, she'll either hate me or hate him. I take the risk and tell her about JC and the girl at the party.

15.

I spend two hours in the hellhole called detention, staring at a whiteboard with the words "No talking" and "No gum chewing" and "No iPods." They might as well add "No breathing" and "No organ functioning" and "No living" on the board, too. My palms are sweaty from the forced silence, and when I check my phone in the hallway, there's a number I don't recognize. Maybe it's Heidi calling from work to thank me for telling her what a true asshole JC is. But there's no voicemail, so I call the number back.

A tired voice answers, "Dr. Confey's office, how can I help you?"

I gulp from the sudden suckage surrounding the fact that Heidi isn't calling. But then I clear my throat. Maybe this is better than Heidi's phone call. Bev's doctor is calling me back.

"One moment," I say, "I'm sorry, just a second." I'm trying to buy some time while I make my way to the stairwell, freaked out that another delinquent from detention will hear me talking to a gender specialist. I whisper, sure I sound like a twelve year old girl. I lower my voice and correct myself as I tell the receptionist who I am and that I'm returning a missed call.

Over the phone, they ask me a few basic questions, and we set up an appointment. Dad has to come, too. I hang up and let out a "hellllllz yeah!" which echoes up to the top of the cement ceiling so it sounds like ten high-pitched Tirzahs yelling hellz yeah, each one starting just a split second after the first person began yelling. I try it again, this time lowering my voice like Troy. Much. Better. As I sneak out of the stairwell, I strut more than usual, carrying myself like I do at the skate park.

The waiting room at Dr. Confey's office looks like a freak show. Even to me. There's a tall man with broad shoulders, sitting with his legs crossed. He's wearing red lipstick and false eyelashes, and all I can think is how hard it must be for him to live like that. It's so obvious that he's a man dressed as a woman. But I know what he feels inside; that's who he really is—a woman. I nod my head at him, and take a seat in a spot two chairs away from him.

Dad opens a book by C.S. Lewis on Renaissance literature. He laughs at the words on the page, but the giggles are exaggerated.

The transvestite man looks at me again. I nod. Then he asks, "You already going through the change?"

"No, not at all. It's my first time here."

"Oh, wow. You just look so much like a boy, I just thought you were already on your way."

Dad looks up from his book and stares at the man. He sighs deeply and goes back to reading.

"I'm sorry," the man says. He picks at some mascara on his fake eyelash. "I shouldn't ask. It's just that if you're here, I thought. Oh. I don't know. That you're on your way."

"I am. On my way," I say, "I just don't know how to get there."

He smiles at my answer. "I'm sure they'll tell you, but there's a big support group where we all meet once a week and talk about anything. Most of all, it's just nice to hang out with people like us. Makes you realize you're not the only one." He points to a flyer on the bulletin board. It says, TransAlliance. Wednesdays at six. Douglass Community Center.

"Awesome, thanks," I say. And then a nurse calls my name. As I get up to leave my spot in the waiting room I look back at the guy. "You have nice legs," I say. "Really."

He presses his lips together as if to hold his words inside. Then he says, "I appreciate that," and sits up a little taller.

The doctor's visit is a huge blur of technical terms and medical language, and I feel kinda sick. Especially after the surgery talk. I'm nowhere near ready for surgery, and I guess I have to go through almost a year of therapy, and then there are testosterone shots and small procedures.

In the car on the way home Dad looks sick. "Tirzah, really, this is a huge decision, and I'm not sure what you're thinking, but I think maybe you should wait. Illinois University practice starts soon, and that's a girls' team. They're not going to let you on as a boy. You know what happened with that one track star we were talking about the other week."

"Yeah, but she had male genitalia inside her, Dad. She wasn't transgender."

"Alright. But still. I'm not sure if you're old enough for this yet. I mean, when I was graduating high school, I wanted to become a Buddhist and live in Tibet. Thought I'd study over there. But then six months later I met your mother, at a community college, and we both applied to Illinois University together. And both got accepted. That was the end of my life as a Buddhist."

"Religion has nothing to do with your body. It's an outer thing. I'm trying to fix me, not what I believe in."

"No. I get that. It's just that you'll see how much you'll change your mind in the next four years. Everything you like now, you won't like later."

There's no way he's going to understand this. "They said I was old enough, remember, Dad? You were right there with me."

He shakes his head in agreement.

"So maybe there's another way for me to play, oh, I don't know. I mean look at Keats."

"Still infatuated with that butterfly thing, huh?" Dad asks. "Makes me proud." We're stopped at the sign by Serendipity Ice Cream.

The whole time I'm thinking that there's got to be another answer for me. And somehow I'm going to find out. Life can't be all about suffering, right?

"So what about Keats?" Dad gets back into the convo

once he's two blocks from our house.

"Oh, nothing. Just that didn't everyone say he couldn't write 'cuz he was young and didn't study poetry or whatever?"

"Yeah, he was really young. Talented as hell, though."

"Like Justin Bieber?" I laugh at our inside joke.

Dad taps the break like he's going to stop. "How you can even use Justin Bieber and John Keats in the same sentence, I have no clue." A Beatles song comes on the radio and Dad turns it up, humming to sixties happiness.

Dad stares out the window at the final stop sign before our house. For three long, silent minutes we sit listening to the Beatles, watching the world from his car like two storm chasers waiting for a tornado to spiral out of the clouds.

"Yeah," he shakes his head. "OK. Why don't you spend a year seeing a therapist, reading more about the treatments, and talking to others? Then we'll consider it. Later. But first, take it slow. Let's get through your first year of college. This is what we've always wanted. Me and you. At Illinois University together!" He bangs his hands on the side of the steering wheel. "Magnificent things are ahead. Just wait!" I sink into the passenger seat. Waiting.

16.

Friday, I was nervous to see Mom, but we had plans to go to some new French restaurant where the celebs hang. I didn't want to pass on a chance at getting some good pics for my Facebook page.

Mom was waiting in the terminal, ending a call on her cell when I approached.

"Oh. My. God." She put her hand on the side of my head. "What happened? Oh Tirzah? What were you thinking?"

"Stop it, Mom. It's nothing to cry over. I just cut it, that's all. Sick of the long stuff."

Mom checks her phone and starts to walk toward the escalator.

I follow and suffer in our silence.

In a cab, she says, "Um, maybe we should just eat at home tonight, huh? How about that?"

"Fine. That's fine. Whatever," I say, hoping she'll notice that I'm disappointed. I'm not as upset about missing the restaurant. It's more about the fact that I can tell she doesn't want to be seen with me. That hurts the most.

"I can wear a hat, you know. And this is just temporary. I was trying something new."

"I hate it," she snaps. "You don't even look like my daughter anymore. You look like a boy. It's like I don't even know who you are." The cab stops in front of Mom's building. A few people stare at us in the lobby. They half-smile at Mom.

In the elevator she says, "Is this why you didn't want to come see me last weekend? Because you're bald now and you knew I wouldn't accept it? I mean, what about college, Tirzah? Do you think they're gonna want a goalie who looks like a freak?" I bite down on my lip and try not to cry. I'm not even going to respond.

We eat with the TV on and I lose myself in some show about home repairs.

"So that's it," Mom says, and finishes chewing her chop suey. "That's what it's going to be like now. You're just going to sit in silence. Just like your father."

I nod my head. The long fohawk part flaps in front of my face.

Mom stands up and tosses her plate in the sink. It crashes like she broke it. "Fantastic!" She says. "Just fantastic. You know what? Just do whatever. I mean, you already do, right? So just keep on transforming yourself into whoever it is you are trying to be. Who are you anyway?"

I take a long time chewing a water chestnut, thinking about Dr. Confey.

I stop eating and look toward Mom who's taking her

hoop earrings out of her ears and putting them in an eclectic glass bowl.

"I just think when God was handing out bodies he mixed up and gave me the wrong one."

Mom walks back to the table and holds on to the back of the tall chair. "What do you mean, the wrong body? You have a gorgeous figure."

Mom takes a seat across the table from me, and I put down my fork. "OK. Do you remember my sixth birthday when you guys asked me what I wanted, and I told you a penis? I wanted a penis for my birthday, Mom." She looks down at her hands and shakes her head in agreement.

"Well then remember when I got my period, and I was, like, depressed for weeks. I just couldn't handle the fact that I really was a girl. I mean, for a while I thought that maybe I wouldn't get my period, but when I did, I just wanted to die. I had this body that I never thought I belonged in. And then I met this woman who used to be a guy. She sells Tupperware now and whatever, but she was telling me all about being transgender and recommended some book. I went to a panel about transgender athletes, and Mom, there's even a chance that I could play on a guy's team somewhere. But I don't wanna spoil Dad's dreams of going to I-U."

"First of all, your father needs to live his own life. But that's totally beside the point here. That man will never learn to live alone." She rubs the top of her hair, raising the poof of blonde to a helmet-sized mass.

I take my plate to the sink. "This isn't about Dad — it's about me."

"Right. OK," Mom sounds both sarcastic and annoyed at the same time. "Let me understand what you're saying here. You really think you're a boy or something? Is that right?" Her fingers find their way back into her hair and she does that behind-the-ear tuck nervous tick that she gets when she can't handle something.

"Yeah. I want to know more, too, but I think that might be why I've hated my body, especially since my period. It's bad, Mom. I haven't told you much. But I hate it something fierce. I want to be a guy."

And then she breaks. Tears fall. She's collapsed her face into her arms. And all I can do is watch, because part of me knows exactly how she feels. Hopeless. And the other part of me feels like frickin' Rocky Balboa, after I just overcame some huge victory. Mom storms off to her room, and I just stare at the home improvement show. A small amount of guilt sits in my stomach, like maybe I've just ruined Mom. But I'm able to block it out and veg in front of the TV.

After four commercial breaks, I could totally faux paint Mom's kitchen based on what I've learned from the show. And maybe that's all I need to get my mind off this shit.

When she walks behind me, heading to the fridge, it's like I freeze. I'm waiting for her to flip.

She grabs a glass and fills it with water from the sink. "God," she says, steadily, her eyes piercing mine. "Maybe having you live with your dad was a mistake. Maybe being around guys all the time has turned you into something that you aren't. I just can't deal with this right now, Tirzah. Whatever crazy mind games you are trying to play with me, just stop already. I'm not Cher and your dad isn't Sonny Bono, and there's no way I'm gonna let my daughter, my baby girl, turn into a guy just because she feels like doing it. Just because some celebrity's daughter did it. No way. Uh-uh." She stares at the TV.

"Son, Mom. It's some celebrity's son," I correct.

A commercial for Mom's newscast airs. "Join Missy Maxon and our news team at ten."

"You look so flipping happy in that commercial, Mom. Like the freaking Febreze lady. But you're really full of shit. Fake as hell!" I scream, and run off to my bedroom, wondering if she'll follow.

But she stays.

Shoving all my clothes in my bag, I leave out a pair of sweat socks. I ball them up real tight and shove them in my underwear. It's hard to pull away from the mirror, at my reflection, a noticeable bump between my legs. I slip on my tightest underwear—just in case the sock comes loose—and throw on a pair of slick basketball shorts.

Leaving my dresser filled with tons of still brand-new girls' clothes I collect my stuff from the bathroom and push past Mom to get to the door. I'm never coming back to her house.

Mom is pressed against the door, her nylon-covered feet slipping on the floor as she freezes in her planted position. "Don't go. Please. Don't." She looks down at my bulge. "Oh, God!" She gasps.

"Too late," I say, and head for the elevator, refusing to look back.

I get over to the park near Mom's condo and pull at the

side of my shirt, itching at the part where I taped my chest too tight. My board drops, sending me up the half-pipe.

On top, C's friend nods his head and gives me a "what up, yo." We knock knuckles, but his stare makes me nervous. It's like he can tell.

I clear my throat. "Sweet pipe you've got here. Wish we had one this tall in the 'burbs."

"Suburbs? Oh, you're the one who's skins with JC, right?" The dude's eyes have that hateful look, like at any moment he could just flip out like some rabid beast.

"Yeah. We're cool. You know him too, huh? He mentioned somethin' like that to me." Shit. I think of that party: Heidi, fucked up, and JC making out with that chick. Still makes me sick.

The rabies guy is in my face. "What's with the look? I mean, you gotta problem or somethin'?" I wait for his mouth to foam.

"No, no nothing like that. I'm just…just thinkin' about this girl back at home."

"Crazy bitches, all of 'em, yo," the dude says and skates off down the ramp. Thank God that's over. It felt like he was onto me, and if he knew I was a "crazy bitch" he would totally kick my ass.

We skate, the whole group of us, for over a half hour. But then my sock starts to move. I'm crouching low to head down the ramp, ready to get some air on the other side. I get to the top, and look down at my package. It's much higher than when it started, and I look like I have a slight boner. But a really high one, like my penis wants to come out of the top of my shorts. Shit. I can't be known as the skater from the suburbs who popped a boner. They'd kick my ass for that, too. With my back to the guys, I pull my shirt down, stretching the cotton, and pretend to tuck in my tank top.

"Dude, why you always touchin' your junk?" The fierce guy says, smacking my back. I jump, startled and scared.

"I think my mom shrunk my clothes, yo," I say. "Seriously, my underwear feels like a dick noose." The dude laughs, loud and obnoxious-like, and I hop on my board and skate away, calling back, "Hey, I'll catch ya later!" I don't wave or look back. I'm outta there.

C catches up with me. "Dude, you should come to this party tonight on Wabash. S'pose to be off the hook."

"Yeah, no, I gotta get home. Only see my mom once in a while. You know how it is." I've had enough drama for the day.

"Cool, yo." C turns back toward the group.

I build speed, getting farther and farther from a near nightmare. I gotta get this sock out of my pants before anything else happens.

There's an underground bathroom at Millennium Park where a crowd has gathered in the music arena. People lounge out under the silver stripes of aluminum or metal or whatever it is that forms such awesome artwork. An orchestra warms up. I skate down a ramp toward the bathrooms, and stomp on my board by the water fountains.

I head into the girls' bathroom, and bump into a plump red-faced woman in a silk shawl. She gasps.

"Sorry," I say. "Excuse me." She looks baffled, and

glances down at my pants. I pull at my t-shirt to cover the sock bulge and scoot off toward a stall.

Thank God for tiny waste boxes in women's bathrooms. I reach into my pants; sweat has saturated my underwear under my belly button. I pull out the balled-up socks that have made their way to the elastic part of my underwear's waistband and toss it in the silver box on the stall wall.

I'm walking out of the bathroom when I hear C and that dude. They're saying, "He's cool, but there's just somethin' that's trippin' me out." I freeze in the open space between the two white cement walls of the bathroom's entrance. Holy shit, they can't see me leaving the girls' bathroom! That'd totally out me. They'd kill me! I inch back toward the sinks and try to listen to their convo, but a young girl runs the air dryer, and I've lost them. I'm thinking about C's friend's words—that I trip him out. Maybe he *does* know.

The little girl at the hand dryer stares at me with a panicked face. "Mama, what's that boy doing in here?" Her mother looks at me sympathetically. She grabs her daughter's hand without an answer, and they exit together.

I stand alone looking at my face and the red circles that have found a home under my eyes from worry, I'm sure. I've gotta fix this. Soon.

When I get back home in the suburbs, Dad has the letter from Illinois University out on the countertop. He's highlighted the words, "impressed" and "full-ride" and "girls' soccer practice starts August 2nd." I skim through it, knowing exactly what I need to do.

17.

Last year I dyed my hair platinum blonde after two straight shut-outs, freaking out wondering if anyone would recognize me. Of course my friends went crazy and loved it. But this Monday is way different. I'm all-out guy now.

I walk down the school hallway with my shoulders wide, arms puffed-up more than normal, and a definite attitude. Fuck what everyone thinks.

Skye's calling my name from behind me, and I ignore her because she's using Tirzah and not Troy. That's the name my mom chose for her daughter based on some fantasy child she imagined who'd spring from her womb reading poetry.

"Tirzah, hey, turn around already!" Skye is so close I can feel her breath on my neck.

I keep my focus straight ahead, but answer, "Tirzah isn't here anymore. You can call me Troy from now on."

She giggles. "Wait, what?" I turn to face her; she continues. "You can't just switch names at the end of senior year. What the hell, T—" I put my fingers to her lips to stop the words.

The hallway feels dim and quiet like everyone is caving in on us, listening.

Skye smiles beneath my fingertips. "I never said I didn't like it, dork. I just don't get how you can show up and—poof!—all the sudden you're Troy. Just kinda drama king, no?"

"Yeah, no." I stop and meet the glances that are focused on Skye and me.

I don't care what anyone has to say anymore.

"I'm sick of holding it in and pretending that there isn't some serious shit going on inside of me that's just dying to get out. And who the hell would understand anyway? Everyone's all perfect with their boy bodies and girlfriends and girl bodies for their boyfriends, but what the hell do people like me do? Are we supposed to hide ourselves forever, smile through some fake mask just so people, what, accept us?" The first hour bell sounds a hollow alarm. The thirty-something people surrounding us stay put. If they want a show, I'll give it.

"I'm a dude, alright. Always have been, and seriously, I don't want any of you calling me any girl's name anymore. It's Troy from now on." I scan my eyes around the group, feeling like freaking Eminem at an open mic, ready to spew and spit my words in beats with rhymes so someone out there will just get me for once.

Skye's face is red like she's about to challenge me, like maybe we are at some open mic. She puts her head down and looks at the blue hall carpet for a moment, then says, "And if you're you, then I'm most certainly me." And she kisses me. In. Front. Of. Everyone.

What's weird is that we're not make-out kissing, but it's more of a tight-lipped kiss. An in-your-face mash. Skye opens her eyes, wide, and we stop.

From the water fountain JC yells, "Goddaaaam!" Everyone laughs a quiet uncomfortable laugh. But it's not like they're making fun of us. It's like they're all standing there searching inside their souls, wondering if they've got anything that wants to come out right now, too.

But no one speaks. And JC kicks in again, "Nothing like a little girl on girl action before first hour!"

Skye smacks my ass. "Girl on guy action, douchebag!" Ashley Lamper with the huge gages in her ears lets out a "Hell yeah!" that starts quietly but gets louder like she's discovered her own voice. Hands clap soft then louder as everyone joins in. And it's like a huge bat mitzvah for Troy, a coming out of girlhood and into guyhood.

But then Heidi comes down the hallway, late from her brother dropping her off. And I freeze.

Mr. Busse shouts at our group, "Get to class already! The bell's about to ring!"

It seems like everyone is whispering about Skye and me, but no one will look at us.

"Mount Ballsmore!" Skye shouts. "Ballzilla! When did you grow a pair?"

"When I took a trip to The Grand Ballsanyon," I answer. "No wait, The Great Balls of China."

Skye is cracking up. "You should open up a fast food restaurant that serves burgers and fries with a side of balls and call it Ballser King."

I let out an insanely loud laugh. "I will," I joke. But really, it's not a bad idea. "Yeah, maybe all the people who can't stand up for themselves, or don't know how to, maybe they'll all visit me at Ballser King and learn how to grow a pair of balls. I'll give 'em a crown just like Burger King if they want."

"We should spell it with a 'z'," Skye says all serious.

"Fo' real, yo," I say.

Heidi closes her locker. "What the hell did I miss?"

"A frickin revolution, Heids," Skye answers.

I want to ignore her after she was such an asshole at lunch, but instead I cave and say, "You didn't miss much." I hate myself for not telling Heidi that something monumental just happened and she missed it. But maybe it was meant to happen that way. Maybe she wasn't supposed to be there because she couldn't handle it.

"K. Moving on," she says and takes a few steps down the hallway. "You'd never believe what my dad did to me now."

What's weird is that I'm not even into listening to her. Did she just catch the fact that something major just went down and all she wants to talk about is herself?

Heidi leans against her locker. "I totally don't want to be here. Wanna ditch?"

"I guess, I mean, I don't have anything major today," I say, putting my books back into my backpack.

"I'm gone, guys," Skye says, "Chemistry test. Can't miss. See ya, Ballzineger."

"Love ya, S," I answer, while Heidi stares blankly at the two of us.

Then she looks at me with those big deer eyes and I'm not mad or anything. Instead, I follow her toward the back of the high school, and out of the field house doors.

We get to my house and I turn up the heat to 72 degrees. It's one of those spring days when Old Man Winter decides to return. Like he hasn't had enough, or he doesn't want us to forget him, so he stops by to remind us how frickin' cold it can get in May. Only in Chicago.

Heidi says, "Let's make screwdrivers. Just little ones, ya know, to celebrate our escape."

"Dude! Are you sure?" I say, worried we'll get caught.

"Hellz yeah, I'm sure. I could totally use some alcohol right now." She starts digging through the cupboard where my dad keeps the booze. Her hand on the vodka, she says, "Mama needs some extra special lovin' this morning."

I grab the orange juice from the fridge and take two clean glasses from the dishwasher. She fills the bottom of the glass with vodka while I pour the juice. "See, we even make good drinks together," I say. "You do one half and I do the other."

"Totally," she says, "only I get to pour the fun half." She takes a huge sip, drinking most of the screwdriver, and pours more vodka. I add more juice to her glass.

With our drinks, we grab some snacks from the pantry and head past the couch where we slip underneath Dad's old army blanket. The one that's nylon and soft, kind of like a parachute. My hand has this weird childish reflex when I hold the blanket: my thumb and forefinger rub together.

Like a picnic in my family room we put the snacks and drinks on the carpet, and sit on the floor.

I'm still holding the blanket when Heidi looks down at my hand. "You gonna suck your thumb, too, *bachcha*?" My fingers are rubbing the soft material together in some freakish reflex like I'm a baby.

I stop my fingers. "What did you just call me?"

"You'll never know, will ya?"

I tickle her for the answer. "What was that, bach-something?" My body becomes tingly from the way her breath feels on my shoulder when she laughs. "Don't make me get all Google on your ass."

We're tickling each other. Laughing that nervous sweaty laugh when your body feels like it's gonna explode 'cuz it's so excited. Then she puts her lips against mine in a long peck. I close my eyes and let her kiss me, hoping she tries to slip her tongue in.

She pulls away. Buzz. Kill. "Hey, I got an idea." She stands up and rubs her fingers on her lips, tracing the spot where my lips were. "'Member when we used to lie by the vents?"

"Totally. God, that was so long ago."

She grabs the can of Pringles and Coco Puffs from the carpet.

We carry the blanket to the corner of the family room, together, and drape the side of it over the heating vent. I lie against the wall; my leg holding the blanket in place. Heidi gets as close as possible and tucks the blanket under her, until we're both beneath the thin layer of nylon.

Nothing happens.

"When's the heat gonna kick on, you think?"

"Soon, I hope," I say, smelling her alcohol-scented breath. We sit in silence, waiting for the air to blast through the vents.

"So I'm thinkin' of running away," Heidi says.

I jerk my head to the side so I can see her face. "Wait. What? I mean, where would you go? And why, your family would—" And then the heat kicks on. The blanket floats up high, and we are underneath a green dome—just Heidi and me—looking up at the top of the blanket. It's like our own piece of the world, heated and all.

"Ahhh, the wonderful Tirz-di-land," Heidi says.

"Holy shit! I totally forgot the name. That's right. That's what we used to call it. Tirz-di-land." This is my heaven. Heidi and warmth and parachute puffiness. Our little bubble.

Then the heat cuts off. And the bubble deflates. And we're almost suffocated by the blanket. It clings to my face, and hers, and we have to put our hands up to keep it off of us.

"This is how I picture it," she says, "when we're old and gray, living in the mountains."

I sit up like I've won some reality show competition. "Old and gray? You want to be old and gray with me?" No way!

She sits up too, and reaches over to grab her drink. After a long sip, she says, "Yeah. You know. Hiking in the mountains, wearing straw hats, using wooden walking sticks." Her lips are wet and loose as she kisses me again. I move my lips slowly, trying to let our tongues touch. But again she pulls away. And now it feels weird. Like why won't she kiss me for real? It's not like it is with Skye where I'm the one who has to pull away.

Then she gets this serious look on her face. "So, I'm gonna leave. Totally sick of this shit. I can't do anything. Can't go on dates. Can't even talk on the phone with guys. Like what? Are we gonna have phone sex or something? Maybe I'll get pregnant by Immaculate Conception and three men can come from Bangladesh bearing gifts. They think I'm sexting. Dad mentioned something about that when he was yelling about my phone calls with JC. Said I was sex-typing. And I was all, wha? And he was like, yeah, you know, typing dirty words with your male friend." She pushes the blanket down to her waist. "Seriously, this has to stop!"

I try to follow what she's saying with my own recap. "Alright. Yes, but dude, if you leave it isn't gonna, like, disappear. They're gonna find you one day. I mean, can't you just have a dinner or something with another family that can explain it to your dad—how hard it is trying to be a teen from another country, struggling to hold on to your culture while trying to fit in. I'm sure there are tons of kids who come from other countries that have a hard time growing up in the U-S. Something's gotta work. Come on. You can't just leave. Right? It's baba, Hafsa."

She holds her stomach. "Don't get all home-school on my now, T. You totally know what I'm going through. Or maybe you don't. I mean, your dad doesn't even look at what you're wearing when you leave the house."

"That's cuz he's totally consumed with his work. And wants to be the cool dad cuz he feels bad about the divorce."

I grab a handful of Pringles and shove them in my mouth. I could eat the whole can right now. Too many crazy things just happened in too short of time.

After a few handfuls of chips, I get the courage to say what I feel. "K. So you know how I totally would do anything for you?"

Heidi's eating Cocoa Puffs, one at a time. "Yeah. Me, too. I would do anything for you."

"Right, but it's different. I think. OK. So this is how I see it. People spend their whole lives looking for that one person to make them happy, right."

She reaches back into the box of cereal and pulls out a tiny mountain of chocolate kernels. A few fall. She picks them up, popping them one by one in her mouth. "Five-second rule."

I hesitate to go on while Heidi crunches on puffs. But I finally say, "So people are always looking for that one person—" I look down at the vent, wondering when the heat will come back on. "You're my happy. It's like I don't know anything else that'll replace the way you make me feel. And, oh, I don't know…"

Heidi throws her hands out in front of her, fingers posed in some mach gang sign. "You're my happy, too, yo. But I'm freakin' miserable cuz the house po-po got me on lockdown." She's totally not ready for this convo.

I switch to gangsta, too: tilt my hat to the left, cross my arms, tucking my fingers beneath my biceps so my muscles look bigger. "But the po-po gotta let their inmates live and breathe a little. See the sun and shit."

"That's what I'm talkin' 'bout, esse." She sucks her cheeks in and gives me a badass look. "Fuck the po-po."

The heat kicks on. We scramble. Lie down. Pull the silky blanket over our heads. Heidi tucks it underneath the side of her left leg. I push the edge of the blanket under my right leg. Together, we've trapped the heat, and the blanket rises. The sun beams through the thin material, and it's like we're underwater, looking up through lighted layers of green.

Heidi closes her eyes and whispers, "This is my happy. Right here." All I want to do is kiss her again, but something stops me. Maybe it's the fact that I don't think she gets how I feel. Her body inches closer, so our clothes are touching from our socks up to our shirts.

The heat shuts off. The blanket deflates, and she's looking at me like she wants to kiss.

I want fresh air. I hate myself for falling into her trap again.

I need to grow some balls. Literally.

"Wanna go for a walk—get out of here for a while?" I ask and stand up. "We could get something to eat."

Heidi pulls her shirt down and tugs at her jeans by her ankles, straightening them. "K. Sure. Down to Serendipity?"

"I could totally go for some Rocky Road." I'm practically salivating over the thought of marshmallows mixed in chunky, chocolatey goodness.

Heidi checks her face in the hallway mirror and looks at me. "Ohhh, Rocky Road. You're so metaphorical."

I grab her coat from the kitchen chair and flick her with it. "You're the one on a rocky road—wanting to run away and all. Seriously, you can't. That's just way too messy."

Heidi swallows hard. "Messy? God you're a dork."

We're walking through the neighborhood with lawns of brownish yellow.

Heidi freezes as a car that looks just like her dad's rolls by. It gets closer and passes.

"Phew!" She whispers. "I just totally thought that was my dad."

"You know what would suck?"

"What?"

"If that really was your dad."

Heidi punches my arm and I push her back. We're two blocks from the small downtown area, in front of a house with tall pine trees. Two plastic deer stand frozen in time, the paint chipping from the taller deer's nose. I run over to the deer and hop on its back. "Giddy up!" I yell, and tap his backside.

"Dude, you're tapping some deer ass right now," Heidi calls out from the sidewalk. "And you're gonna get busted."

I wave her over. "Anyone with plastic deer in their yard probably is, like, ninety years old, drooling through their afternoon nap."

Heidi hops on the other deer and spanks it. Then she makes up a rap song about tapping deer ass that's funny as hell.

She stops so we're both on deer-back staring each other down with that eye gaze where I suddenly forgotten where I am. My lips are quivering like I wanna kiss her.

Then she says, "God you'd be a gorgeous guy."

My heart slips into my throat. "Really? You think?" But why now? How come she wasn't into it before?

She shakes her head yes and leans to the side to dismount the deer.

We're two stores away from Serendipity, its front window covered in posters of little kids eating frozen treats. I have lost my appetite for ice cream. Who needs food when you have love?

"So what's up with that gender doctor?" Heidi asks just outside Serendipity.

Some pre-pubescent crackle attacks my voice when I try to speak. I try again. "Should know more when I go back. Right now I have no idea what the hell's gonna happen. I'm gonna spend more time like this before fully changing. But I totally wish there was medication or something that could fix my problem. I wish there was some pill that they advertised on TV, like the one for erectile dysfunction. Something I could take that would help me change into a guy. What's that one commercial for depression that lists a shitload of side effects?"

"Oh yeah, like, 'this pill could give you seizures or cause you to blackout or make you foam at the mouth.'" She makes a seething sound and her body shakes, her arms jerking, like she's having a seizure.

I yell, "Get a hold of yourself, woman!" and capture her underneath her arms until she stops the act.

When I open the door, an old bell at the top of the door frame haunts our entrance. "Seriously, maybe there's an answer for me," I add.

But then Heidi gasps as we're walking into the ice cream shop.

"Hafsa?" Heidi's brother is paying at the register, holding a bag of nonpareils. His girlfriend stands behind him, her head covered. She smiles at Heidi, and turns her face away from me.

Heidi takes a step back, her hand on the door, ready to escape. "Hamid? What are you doing here?"

Hamid pushes change into his pocket. "Me? Why aren't you at school? Hafsa? What is this?" He points to me. I am "this."

I step in front of Heidi, protecting her from what could get ugly. "We were just—"

Hamid lunges at us and pulls Heidi by the arm. "You're coming with me!" Hamid shouts more in Bangla. The bag of candy falls to the floor, nonpareils rolling everywhere. The little white snowy pieces bounce up and down, the heavy chocolate circles scatter.

Hamid pushes past me and shoves open the door; the bell rings again.

"Thamun! Thamun!" Heidi shouts.

"Don't tell me to stop," Hamid remarks and looks at me in the store's doorway. "You didn't want to listen when baba told you to stop hangin' around her. Now I'm not listening to you." He opens the backseat of his girlfriend's car door, and pushes Heidi in.

"Bi-smi Allah ar-rahman ar-rahim," he recites.

It's like she's being kidnapped by her own brother who's protecting her in the name of God.

18.

Heidi is ignoring my texts. I didn't mean to get all psychotic on her, but when she didn't return one, I kept sending them, thinking maybe she'd get the others. And then when I thought she was mad at me, I sent more. Now she won't return my e-mails. I just want to know that she's alright.

Leaving school on Tuesday, I realize that I spent the day with virtually no comments about my look. And what's weird is that nothing's changed much. It's not like I woke up and highlighted all the tags on my clothes that said Men's size small or Men's size 30. None of that.

I stop home before heading to the skate park and Dad has this worried look on his face.

I meet him in the kitchen where he pours me some coke; he fixes a cup of coffee. We sit in silence for a minute, I check my phone—still nothing from Heidi—while he stirs the coffee in thoughtless circles. "So the school called." He leaves it at that, so I'm stuck deciphering what the phone call might have involved.

"Oh, my detention? I told you about that." The coke

bubbles tickle my nose; my eyes water.

"Nah. Not the detention. I knew about that remember? The e-mail?"

I nod and wait for more.

"Yeah, so," he sits, now physically suffering from something deep inside, like the time when he told me him and mom were gonna split. "Your teachers talked to the dean about your request for a name change. And I understand why you might not have wanted to tell me, but this is a big deal. People can't just ask their teachers to call them a different name." He does that nervous rambling where I know he's still on the same topic so I tune him out, scroll through Facebook, look at the status updates. JC wrote on Skye's wall, "Suck for a Buck." I giggle, but am kinda jealous that the two of them are Facebooking each other all the sudden.

Dad stands up, forces his chair into the table. "That's enough hiding behind that crap, Tirzah. Turn it off!" He takes my phone and I hear the fading signal warning me that my phone has been shut off.

"What? What do you want me to say, Dad?" I stand up so we're face to face. The spot beneath his eyes are red, veins popping out.

"I want you to tell me what's going on."

And so I do. Let him know that I've asked the teachers to call me Troy. I told them ahead of class that I'll be going by Troy from now on. No one said much but my chemistry teacher who looked super uncomfortable. He's a dick anyway, so I didn't expect anything less.

What sucks is that Dad looks like he is about to cry. He takes a deep breath and flips through a National Geographic on the table. But I keep thinking about Ballser King. If I'm gonna be a king, I can't just try on a crown when I feel like it. I've gotta keep it on. Always.

"I get that you're upset, Dad. I get it. But just bear with me for a while and I think it'll work out. Somehow, right."

Dad looks helpless, but I remember some of the other people on the panel saying the same thing. It takes time.

19.

High school feels like the loneliest place on earth without Heidi. She's been out for three days now. I'm so tempted to just drive to her house, but I'm afraid her brothers will kidnap me and hide me in a place where their sister will never find me.

After second period, JC stares at me kind of weird like from the other side of the hall.

I'm not in the mood. "Fuck? Whatcha lookin' at?" I check myself in the locker mirror. My eyes are all puffy and bloodshot. My two front teeth have this white slimy stuff coating them, and I wish I wasn't so hungover. Maybe I would have remembered to brush. Vodka's a bitch in the morning.

JC sneaks up next to me, checking himself in the mirror, but then he backs away. Quickly. "Shit, Maxon, what'd ya eat — ass for breakfast?"

I blow my breath in his face. "Naw. I'm sorry, man. I've just been dealin' with a lot right now. Can't get my head on straight."

"Yeah. Hey. Where's Heidi been? Have you talked to her?"

"Not at all," I say, half-relieved that it wasn't just me. "Can't seem to catch her online. She's not chatting. No texts. Nothing."

"Dude. What happened?" He asks, moving me out of the way so he can check himself in the mirror again. I've never seen someone so in love with himself before.

I get all raging mad, like the Vodka is resurfacing again. "Fuckin' brother found us ditching the other day. Took her away and that was it. Never heard from her again."

JC steps away from my locker and looks blankly down the hall at a group of girls in their typical pre-bell panic—cramming gossip in between class periods. Then he says, "She sent some message on Monday sayin' her parents totally wigged out. They're gonna hold her out of school this week and shit."

I'm so pissed right now. "Is that even legal? I mean, can they just pull her out of school like that?"

"Probably, yeah. They're her parents and all."

The bell rings and we head for Home Ec. "Lemme know if she sends you another message," I say. JC shakes his head.

I can't believe she didn't send me one. Why him and not me? That's total bullshit. I mean, I'm the one always there for her, taking care of her, and he's the one that dicked her around.

I get home from school and before taking my coat off I head to Dad's office to check e-mail. There are a bunch of messages from stores and crap, and then one from Heidi.

Mom's in the bathroom. I have one sec. Miss you. Uh. Hell. Can't talk to anyone. They think you're trouble. I tried to tell them it was my idea to ditch, but they blame you. I'm gonna keep trying to convince them. Miss you. Love you. Hopefully see you soon. Wait. I'm working Sat. 4-7. Come by. Xxxxoooooo, H

I type back.

It'll be OK. Everything's just sucks without you. Maybe I could talk to your parents or something. Maybe they'd understand I'm not some brain-washing alien child trying to take over their daughter. Yeah, I'll see you at work! Can't wait!!! Luv ya lots, me

Relief! I can see her in two days. But why am I always the one being blamed?

Just the thought of knowing she's OK and that I'll see her soon makes me sleepy. I can finally relax. She's OK. I am so tired that the words on the computer look like jklsdjfwoeriuoweruwsdklfjlsdj.

20.

I'm super sweaty and the road looks like a videogame screen. I'm trying to fight my way through the lazy Saturday drivers to get to Partytime, ready to blast people out of the way with my laser-horn. Damn I should have slept last night instead of thinking about what it'd be like if Heidi and I were living together forever in the mountains, wearing handmade hats while hiking by waterfalls.

I get in the store and walk past the life-size Robert Pattinson cutout. Heidi's behind the counter, helping some woman. She hands her a bunch of turquoise balloons with the words "50 is Nifty!" I stay by Cardboard Robert and watch Heidi finish up with the lady.

With deep purple lips and her hair pulled back she looks like someone sucked the life out of her. It's like she doesn't even care enough to wear makeup anymore. But she's still beautiful. You could cover Heidi in uglysauce, put nasty ripped clothes on her, make her hair all crazy and ratty, and she'd still look pretty.

I keep my spot next to Cardboard Robert. And then I

think of this conversation Heidi and I had a while ago after the midnight opening of Eclipse. If we had kids, like if there was any way it was possible, we'd name our son Edward. We'd let his hair grow out on top and, yeah, we'd even buy him a binky that looked like vampire teeth.

And then my heart feels like it's gonna break. Even though Heidi is there, and she's pressing buttons on the register, and I'm only eight feet away from her, I just know there's no way any of our dreams are ever gonna come true. There's no way her parents are ever going to forgive me. Never. I just know it. I almost want to leave. Why stay and get my heart broken by being close to her for just a few hours and then say goodbye—not knowing when I'll see her again?

But then the customer leaves, and Heidi comes out from behind the register. She picks up a plastic guitar and puts this crazy wig on her head that looks like one of those nineties hair bands. Grabbing dark black sunglasses from a tall rack, she pushes them on her face.

She starts banging her head, pretending to play the guitar. "Meh, meh, meeeeaaah!" She fake sings, sounding like the howling voice of an old metal band.

"Aerosmith?" I ask.

Heidi's fingers are going crazy, fake strumming on her blow-up guitar. "Berrrn, ner, ner, ner, ner, neeeeeer!" She squeals.

"It's more like this," I say, and take the blow-up guitar and make strange high-pitched squeals.

Heidi is cracking up. Her long wig gets sucked into her laughing mouth. She hugs me. "God, I miss you."

"Me, too." My eyes close and I pretend like we're on stage, just us in our very own hair band.

I open my eyes as a college-age girl leans against the register. "Hey, that's, um, really cute and all, but maybe you could play dress-up when you get off work."

We drop our arms and lose the hug. Heidi takes the glasses off, and pulls the wig from her hair. She's glowing again. "Sorry, Latanya. It's just that I haven't seen her in a while."

"No biggy. But let's get this place straightened up so we can close quickly and get out of here."

"Got it," Heidi says, and looks at me with these really sad eyes. "Wait one sec." She sifts through the latex balloon bins, pulls two out, and sneaks behind the counter.

She wraps the tip of the balloon around the air nozzle. It makes a loud hissing sound. I watch the first red balloon expand. It says, "Be Mine." She twists a knot around the bottom and attaches a long silver string to it.

She pulls at the second balloon, a gorgeous blue. Big white letters expand on the latex, stretching the words "Baby Boy." Heidi ties another silver ribbon at the bottom of the blue balloon, and she hands me the red one first. Be mine. She's silent, but her eyes tell me hours of stories. Baby Boy. She does this weird thing with her mouth where it twitches, kind of like a bunny moving its whiskers. Her eyes get glassy; I don't want her to cry at work.

I stare at the balloons: Be Mine. Baby Boy. I wonder if this is her way of saying she finally wants us to be together.

I can't handle her crypticness right now, so I grab a pen

from next to the register and take a piece of scratch paper. I write, "Fo' shniz," and pass her the note, playing along with her silent message game—whatever it means. Her lips form a huge smile, and she makes a small wave with her hand.

I'm not sure if I should go, but Latanya is giving us the worst looks.

I don't know when I'll see her again, so I say, "Tell baba I miss him." Heidi's face goes soft and sad. I continue, "I'm sure he'll come around, though. Look. Growing some hairage back." I rub my head, feeling the stubble from the outgrowth like prickly carpeting. I'm still lingering in the spot between the register and the door.

In an aisle of pirate decorations, Heidi straightens some eye-patches. She says, "No. He really does dig you. He's just pissed. It's so much more than you and me and whatever we told him or didn't tell him. It's his job, too. They're cutting two docents from the museum—not enough funding—so he's freaking out, like it could be him. Then my grandpa is not doing good so he wants to go see him and wants us all to go. This sucks. See that's why I've been holdin' out on you through e-mail. How the hell am I supposed to tell you that I'm leaving?"

It's like some messed up dream where I'm falling, about to hit the pavement. She did not just say what I thought she said, right?

"Tirzah?!"

Why the hell can't she just call me Troy?!

Latanya has been Windexing the same part of the counter the whole time we've been talking, and the store is beginning to smell like a carwash.

She squirts and wipes. "Really, you're gonna have to finish up now. Seriously, Heidi, we've gotta start closing."

"That's cool. I'm sorry," I say to Heidi's boss. "Heidi, just get your parents to let you come back to school. I wanna see you on Monday. Tell them whatever you have to. And we'll talk then." I'm opening the door, but stop to say one more thing. "Please don't leave. You gotta stay. Seriously, it'd be a helluva long flight to go see you. You can't go. Not when we're almost eighteen. Come on! Seriously. I can't take this and I don't want this. And why does this have to happen now when I need your support the most?" This is what she's reduced me to—a pouting baby, whining and fighting for attention.

Heidi comes out from around the counter and picks up some random bouncy balls and blowy things that got knocked on the floor; she puts them back. "I don't have much choice. Really it's all up to my dad. I'm stuck, T. Totally at his mercy."

"Then you're gonna have to kiss his ass for, like, ever. Just tell him whatever it takes. And I'll be seein' you Monday. Got it?"

"Yup," she says, and she presses her lips together, like she's about to cry. "No worries. I should see you—" Tears fall, but she tries to hold it together. "You'd better go though. My mom'll be here soon."

There's something about watching the person you love cry that hurts in worst places. I try to fight my tears, but it's no use. My car starts, and for a moment I want to drive right through the store window and rescue Heidi. With glass falling all around us, we could reverse out of there and keep driving until we ran out of gas. Then we could live wherever my car took us. Out in the wild. Together.

Then I see her mom's car approaching from the street. Signaling to turn into the strip mall. I back out of my parking spot as fast as I can.

Mrs. Chaudhary pulls into Partytime's lot, but I'm already in another parking lot. Hiding out near some craft store I take a moment to breathe.

21.

"I can't believe it's like that. I mean, how'd they find out about the party anyway? And the Special K?" Skye and I are in the locker room Monday morning, changing for gym. And, no, there's nothing weird between us. Even after that night.

"I told you last night, her brothers printed all her old e-mails. One of 'em had this whole apology between her and JC about the Special K. I guess she totally forgave JC for leavin' her side." Skye sits on the bench and ties her shoe.

"But your IM's were so vague, dude. So, wait, she, like, had a bunch of e-mails between her and JC, and she totally forgave him. And. She never deleted them?"

"Yeah. But her brothers printed 'em for her parents, and then there was this huge thing about her taking drugs. And they totally blame you 'cuz you said you'd take care of her. You said you'd take her to the movies. You said she was alright when she was sleeping at your house." My god. I totally hate Skye right now and want to tape her mouth shut or something after watching her say all those terrible things.

Like doesn't she get that it was Heidi, not me, who did all those things?

Just this once, I wanna kill the messenger.

"Fuck. Alright already." I slam the locker shut so hard that it makes my eyes blink. "This is such bullshit. I'm not a bad person, and they're making me out to be the bad guy."

"Give it time, T, and they'll get over it."

"I don't have time. I'm leaving soon. We don't have that much more time together."

"This is such craziness," she says. The bell rings for PE to start and we're still in the locker room, which means we're now tardy. Major suckage.

We enter the gym and Rip scribbles something in the attendance books.

I give him a look. "Please. Not. Today."

He erases.

So basically, the only way I'm gonna be able to see Heidi is if, um, I disguise myself as a Bangladeshi male. Which is definitely not going to happen. School gets out in a week. How am I going to convince Heidi's dad that I'm not some freaking monster out to corrupt his daughter? Then I only get six weeks of summer before I'm heading to Illinois University for summer training. Coach Shoals has sent three e-mails already saying I'm his new star goalie. There was even something in the college paper about it. Yeah, no pressure or anything.

The thing about getting caught is that all the feelings you hid from return and it hurts twice as bad. It sucked having to lie to Heidi's parents the first time, but now that they know what really went down, I feel like such an asshole. I'm the one who screwed up their perfect image of their daughter. I'm the one who helped her get into all that shit with JC. If I didn't cover for her, she would've been screwed. And safe.

All I can do is imagine Heidi sitting at dinner in silence while her father stares her down like she betrayed their entire family.

I've gotta talk to her again. They can't just break us up forever! Can they?

22.

I am an exoskeleton of teenage nothingness waiting to shed my skin like one of those annoying cicadas. Wouldn't that be cool? If I could just hide up in some tree and my girl-skin would just fall to the ground so I could emerge as a guy. Dude. Bugs have it so easy and they don't even know it.

Dad and I head home from grabbing stuff from the food store, and now everything looks brighter: houses, people, even that one rundown deli on the corner that looks like it'll topple over any moment, and who would want a turkey sandwich from that place—even that place looks brighter today.

We're on our street, in front of Mrs. Baxter's house with the purple flower-lined walkway. There's something hanging from the antennae of my car. I freak.

Closer, I see that it's a balloon waving in the wind. We're two houses away and every second seems like forever until we pull in the driveway. I know it's from Heidi, but I can't see what it says.

Dad pulls in the driveway, and before the car is in park,

I'm hopping out to read Heidi's message.

White letters spell out the phrase "Bon Voyage" with confetti surrounding the words. I pull at the red string to get the balloon loose, looking for another message. There's a tiny slip of paper pressed into the hood of my car. "Fair Oaks," it says. And that's it.

"I'm gonna be back in a bit, Dad. Going to see if Heidi's at work."

Dad's already heading to the front door, carrying two paper bags filled with food and a gallon of milk. "You sure that's a good idea. Her father wouldn't mind you visiting his daughter at work?"

I've started my car, but we're still talking through the rolled-down window. There's nothing that he could say to stop me. "It'll be fine. No worries. Be home in a bit." I'm down the driveway, waving goodbye, and ignoring his hesitation.

Fair Oaks Park is packed with Saturday picnickers, and I have no idea where to find Heidi in this five mile space. I follow the rock path toward the hill where we had our balloon race. There's a balloon tied to a yellow dog walking sign. Another Bon Voyage balloon. I keep going. She must be up the path somewhere.

I'm in a spot on the path where the sun shines through the trees, lighting them up. It's quiet and haunting at the same time, and I start to wonder what Heidi did. Or why she's leading me into the forest.

I've walked for twenty minutes, following the path

without finding another balloon. What if something happened to her? Or she did something stupid? I look down the forest path for any sign of her, but only see fast running squirrels and moss covered tree stumps.

It's spooky-quiet when I start to climb a hill. Branches snap in the distance. My head snaps toward the sound. Twenty feet away, a deer hops over a long log and runs in the opposite direction of me.

I'm ready to give up my search, and call the police because this is so unlike Heidi. She would never trick me or lure me into the forest without being there. But something keeps me going. I head further down the path as the sun is setting and find a silver balloon tied to a tree branch off in a clearing. Which way am I supposed to go? I can't play this mind game anymore. What if Heidi's really hurt?

"Heidiiiiii!" I call out in the open air. Birds fly from their resting places. "HEEEEIDIIII!" I yell even louder.

There's a faint answer, from where I can't tell, but I keep down the path. She's out here somewhere.

I step over fallen trees, twigs, and plants that look like poison ivy, heading in the direction that I heard Heidi's voice. She hasn't answered me in a few minutes, and I know she's screwing with me.

The maze of green is brown is so disorientating. And when the sun almost disappears, it becomes freaky quiet. My heart pounds as I look up in the trees for Heidi.

Out of nowhere she jumps down from a thick tree branch. "Funky Fresh!" She yells, holding out the plastic monkey. I think she's fucked up.

We hug tight, and I pull back to look at her face to see if she's alright. Her eyes are all wide and big and glassy. "What are you doing here? What's this all about?"

"I'm done. Not gonna put up with it anymore. Don't need it anymore. So I just left." She stumbles back on a log.

"Whadya mean, left?"

She reaches for her backpack, lying at the base of the tree. "I packed some shit, and took off. Me and some balloons. Left you clues, 'cuz you're the only one I wanted to be with." She digs through her backpack and pulls out a bottle of water. "I'm thirsty as hell."

"Wait. So how long'r you plannin' on stayin' out here?"

"Shit. I don't know. Who cares? Right? All that matters is right now." She leans in again for another hug, and I'm done. I'm gone. All the things I want to say, like the part of my brain that would tell me this was so wrong, are gone. I'm mush.

We sit there together on the log, and I listen to Heidi's stories about how she spent so many years trying to make it at school where she was always so different from everyone. How she wanted to wear what everyone else was wearing, but was always fighting her father on what he thought was appropriate. And what's so weird, is that we're more alike than I ever knew. She doesn't blame her family; she blames society.

There are a million stars above us, and the moon glows super bright. It's like heaven with Heidi and me and our own little place in the world.

She puts her pinky out, and I move my hand toward hers. We join pinkies together, and flap our hands like a butterfly. Maybe I'll finally get my three summer days with her. But then what?

Heidi undoes a sleeping bag, lays it on the ground, and pulls a tiny pillow from her backpack. "It feels so good to get away from them. Get away from everything. We don't need anything else, right?"

"Dude. This is so *Into the Wild*. But you know what happened to that guy. I don't want to eat the poisonous plants and die and shit. We can't stay here forever."

Heidi pats the sleeping bag for us to climb in.

"Shhhh," she says, putting her finger to my lips. My insides flip. My eyes roll back a little. She kisses me. I'm hypnotized by the way she moves her tongue. My heart gets this warm feeling like I could live forever—never sleeping— just as long as I had Heidi under the treetops.

We slip in the sleeping bag, lying shoulder to shoulder, looking up at the stars. I kiss her neck, ready to move down, but she's out of it. Whatever she's taken has her so knocked out that she falls right asleep. My mind races as I wiggle back to my spot in the sleeping bag. There's no way I can leave her here alone, but I've gotta tell my dad where I am. But if I tell Dad where I am, then he'll tell her parents. Shit.

I shut off my phone so he can't find us. Then I bury my head in Heidi's shoulder. I try to sleep. Toss and turn. Sleep on my right side. Sleep on my left side. Nothing works. Heidi is out cold, and I'm wide awake, thinking about Dad being worried.

I've spent an hour wondering if he'll come looking for me. Or worse, send the police out looking for my car. He would, too. This totally sucks. We're alone in the woods in our own paradise, but I can't sleep. If this is going to work, I'm going to have to get rid of my car so no one will find us. And then I keep thinking about soccer and I've gotta make a decision soon. I could be a coach or something someday. My head's gonna explode.

Without waking Heidi, I slip out of the sleeping bag, and make my way back to my car. I'll wait until Dad's asleep and then have HP drive me back.

The walk back takes forever, and when I reach my car there's an officer looking inside of it.

"This your car?" asks a man with a Smoky the Bear hat. Not the police, thank God.

"Yeah. I'm sorry. I got lost on a hike. Didn't think I'd get out of those woods."

He's looking at me strange. "You by yourself?"

I hesitate. "Yep. Just me. What time is it anyway?"

"Almost ten. Park closes at nine. I was about to lock the entrance gate when I saw your car. Was about to call it in."

"Oh. No need to do that. I'm fine. See. Just lost."

He's still checking me out. I try to calm my breathing. "Alright," he says, "next time you better carry a phone or something. We've had problems with coyotes. Not that they'll touch you, but they like dogs."

I laugh nervously. "Oh. Well, no, I don't have a dog. But thanks for the info. Again. Sorry." I find my keys in my pocket and slip into my car. The guard waves as I pull out. Coyotes? Even if they only eat dogs, I still wonder if they'll bother Heidi. I've gotta hurry back.

I get home and Dad is working in his office. He gets up the minute he sees me. "I tried to call, you know, but you had your phone off. Everything alright?" His shirt is untucked and the buttons on his sweater are one-off.

"Fine. I just went to Ty's to skate," I say, and hope it's enough for him. Then I add, "Had a lot on my mind. Lots to think about."

"But didn't Heidi leave that balloon? I thought you guys weren't talking anymore."

I gulp and quickly think. "Ty was just screwin' with me. He stopped by Heidi's work just to play a joke on me." And then I tell Dad some stupid story about Ty and me playing Star Wars on our skateboards where he was Darth and I was Luke, and we battled with saber swords on our boards. And everything's fine. Any mention of anything Star Wars and Dad geeks out. It's a sure thing.

Things are calm on the home front, and Dad heads up for bed, like, an hour after I get home. HP is out for the night at some motocross race.

When I think Dad is truly asleep, like in a deep sleep where he won't get up for the bathroom or whatever, I open my window and pull in the screen from my window and leave it against my wall. Dad will never find it since my door's locked. Even if he wanted to check on me in the middle of the night, he'd need that tiny screwdriver to pick my lock. Not gonna happen.

Leaving a small space of window open, I hold on to the deck so I'm kinda like a lemur, on all fours. There are five inch spaces between each plank of wood, and I'm freakin', wondering what would happen if my foot slipped through. I get to the edge of the deck roof, and hang from my hands until my foot touches the deck's side rail. I made it!

It's pitch dark outside except the glow from the street lights. A dog barks from inside my neighbor's house as I walk by, and it freaks me out. I don't want anyone to see me walking by myself late at night. I've got a long way to go until I get back to the park. This time, I'm prepared for a night in the woods with a flashlight and granola bars, some bread, and chips. Pop. Bug spray. I've got it taken care of. I even grabbed HP's Swiss Army knife in case we need to cut wood or something. This is so Survivor.

The worst part about the walk back to the woods is that I have to follow the train tracks and stay away from the roads. If the cops caught me by the street, they'd take me home. Plus, I'd be busted for curfew.

The tracks are the loneliest place in the world. No animals. No bugs. No sticks. No trees. Just iron stripes in the ground that go on forever, and rocks as lonely as I am. I take the middle of the tracks, stepping on every other wood plank. I'm worried about Heidi all by herself on the forest floor. There aren't many snakes here, but we have a few. And what if they bite Heidi? Or what if someone's lurking in the forest? And she's so out of it.

I start jogging so I get there faster. And then I'm running. Full speed. The tracks below look like they're moving in the darkness.

I climb over the yellow barricade to get in to the forest preserve. It's peaceful and beautiful and my heart rate slows down knowing I'm close to Heidi. The air is heavy and moist, calm and quiet. But then I hear howling.

Running down the path, I clutch the pocketknife, hoping the coyotes want nothing to do with me. The rocks scatter as my feet hit the trail until I finally find Heidi, curled in a ball.

After a few sips of water, I take off my shoes and pants and slip into the sleeping bag with Heidi. She makes a tiny mumbling sound and moves over a little. Man, she must've taken more than one sleeping pill. She's out cold, but her body is super warm. I put my face back in the spot where it was before I left. Her neck is a little sweaty, but I can still smell my happiness.

23.

The birds wake us. Heidi opens her teary eyes. "I thought I'd never see you again," she says, with her hand over her mouth. "Morning breath. Sorry," she whispers.

I giggle. "You saw me yesterday, whadya mean?"

"No, I thought I'd never see you again, so I left home."

There's this rush in my chest, blood pumping into my heart. "Wait," I say, "You said you left cuz your parents and everything else. Not cuz of me."

"I mean, mostly cuz of my parents not wanting me to see you again" She goes on to tell me how once I shaved my head her dad thought I was majnun. And then all that stuff about the e-mails comes up again. I'm sick from thinking about it.

With my eyes closed I try to block out the rest of her story about how her parents hate me.

Then I tell her about the ranger and how I had to leave last night. I finish, "We'd better pack our stuff up and move or something. Don't want that ranger to find us." I climb out of the sleeping bag, and put my pants back on.

Heidi sits up, still slow moving. "Man I was out of it. Didn't even notice you left."

"Huh! I know. Crazy."

We finish getting dressed, clean up, and head for the path. Walking in the direction of the sun through an open part of the forest. There's nothing around to worry about and no one else to get in the way; life is perfect. If only it could stay this way forever.

We find a tree with several giant limbs that reach out at different levels like arms: one is a foot off the ground, another several feet higher, and then another limb is ten feet in the air.

"Suh-weet! This is like a freakin' ladder or something!" Heidi climbs on the first limb, and then keeps going until she's at the top of the tree. "Oh my God, I can see across the whole forest! This is the best!" She calls from the highest branch.

I follow her up there until we're both on the same limb. Heidi inches toward the base of the tree. Her back leaning against its bark. "Look, Huck. I've got my own lil' recliner." She says in a weird southern accent.

I play along, a gangsta Huck Finn. "Yuz crazy big pimpin', Jim! Imma be livin' up in the tree forevah, homie!"

We keep on for a while, gangsta-izing lines from *Huck Finn*, still fresh in my head from the test in English class. Then I get stuck laughing so hard that I forget I'm up, like, a gazillion feet in the sky. I lean back and almost lose my balance—almost fall off.

Heidi grabs my arm, and yanks me toward her so she's

holding my upper body in her lap. "Shit! You just gave me a heart attack!" She shouts.

"No shit. What if I fell? Oh my god. That'd suck ass." We're laughing again. More this time because it's like we're cheating life.

We sit on a log by the side of the pond and watch night fall. The bugs sing around us, avoiding our skin drenched in strong smelling anti-bug perfume.

Heidi looks at me all funny. "What?" She tilts her head. "Whatcha thinkin'?" She picks through her backpack and pulls out a reading light, book, and a package of Twizzlers, handing me one. "Just that I've got all I need right here."

I take a bite of my Twizzler and talk through my chewing. "I would live here with you forever. I could totally see us doing it. And maybe not in these woods. Maybe we'd have to go somewhere warmer, but we could do it. Backpacking our way to paradise. But then there's that thing called my future. Shit. I've gotta get back home to check in with Dad before he gets all worried. But I'll come back as soon as I can."

She looks like she's going to cry.

Two ducks approach the water in front of us, their feet are dark shadows dangling and flapping like air brakes. They land together, touching water at the same time. "Or not," I continue. "Or maybe I could stay here and we could live like this—just me and you—and hope my dad just forgets about me. Like, what? I had a daughter who's really my son? Naaaah. Couldn't be. I haven't seen any daughter around here lately. Last I know I almost had two sons. Maybe one and a half sons. And half of a daughter. That's hard to explain."

"Alright, crazy. Why don't you go home now and come back later. Sneak out again. And then we'll have all night to think about it. Figure out what to do. It'll be fine. Don't worry. I'll be fine."

"You sure?"

"Yep. Positive." She gives me a long hug and I walk away. When I turn back to see her, she opens her pill bottle, pops some, and then climbs up the tree with the book and reading light.

"I'll just read up here 'til you get back. This way I can see if anyone's coming."

She's almost on the high branch when I say, "Gimme a couple of hours."

"Miss you," she says, all cute-like.

I walk fast, hoping I'll hit the pavement soon so I can hop on my board.

Far down the path, I can still see the glow from her book light from high up in the tree.

24.

When I get back home Dad's wrinkles are carved deeper in the space between his eyebrows. "You're beet red. Where were you all day?"

I take off my hoodie, all wet from sweat. "I was at the park with Ty. Ran into a bunch of guys and had a sort of mini-tournament."

"Thank God you're off to college soon. I'll feel better knowing you're somewhere on campus rather than who-knows-where." He slips back into his office. "I've been taping up boxes all day, getting some of this stuff packed up now so we're not killing ourselves later. Your brother did most of this, and he's not even moving."

I make Dad happy with some more small talk and then head upstairs. "I'm beat. Think I'll just shower and go to bed."

"Good thinkin'. Better get your rest." The duct tape roll makes a loud whining sound as Dad keeps working downstairs.

After my shower, I put on comfy track pants and a t-shirt, slip under my covers, and lie in bed trying to ignore the knots in my stomach.

Twenty minutes later, footsteps tap on the stairs. I listen as Dad runs the water, flushes the toilet, and mumbles something. The house is quiet except for night sounds from outside my window.

I wait until Dad is totally out. After tying my shoes and shoving my board in my backpack, I'm out the window.

As I'm leaning the screen against my bedroom wall and sliding the window shut except for a small crack, my door knob jiggles.

My heart races as I try to climb back inside before they can get in my room. I bang my knee on the metal window ledge. It kills. Throwing my backpack on the ground, I leap for my bed, kicking off my shoes while Dad says, "Tirzah, why is your door locked?" He's speaking softly, which is weird 'cuz if he's trying to wake me up why is he whispering?

I rub my eyes so they look red and tired. Still, I don't answer.

"Open up, Tirzah. Right. Now." He rattles the door handle. "Oh. Right. Are you ignoring me because I'm not using your new alias? Is that it?" More rattling.

Jumping to the door, I unlock it and meet my panicked father face-to-face. The air feels weird like we're outside, but really we're inside. And then I look toward the open window.

Dad follows my glance so we're both staring at the open window and the screen against the wall.

Dad walks over to the window and sticks his head out

into the night sky. He looks left and right. "What were you doing here? Smoking or something?" I think what might happen if I tell him I was smoking. He'd probably have a conniption, but it's easier than telling him what's really up.

I hesitate. "Ummm. Yeah. I was smoking. But I never really smoke, and I don't even like to smoke, and I was just trying it cuz I'm so stressed about moving and leaving and worrying about Heidi. I'm sorry. Really, really sorry." I try to get my eyes to tear up a little.

"You know what Tirzah? You can't be a good goalie while you're pumping carcinogens into your body. Never gonna happen. You have to stop." I wait for him to lean forward and smell my breath or look around for a box of cigarettes. But he doesn't. He just walks out of my room without saying another word. As if the words I said hurt him so badly that he can't talk about it anymore.

My heart still races as I try to fake sleep.

Dad comes back. "Keep your door open tonight," he says before turning to leave.

But Heidi's up in the tree reading and waiting for me.

If I try to sneak out and get caught, who knows what Dad will do? All the negative stuff about getting in trouble makes me think what Heidi might do if I don't show up. She could totally call someone else to meet her in the forest. What if she calls JC and they get to spend the night together while I'm here worrying about her? After all, he was the one who basically made her parents hate me in the first place. It wasn't just my shaved head. It was JC taking her out. What if she still doesn't feel the way I feel about her? What if this is a sign? Like I'm not supposed to go back there. What if right this very moment the two of them are wrapped underneath our sleeping bag and he's touching her and she's liking it?

Maybe my dad catching me before I left is the best thing that ever happened to me. What if someone's trying to tell me to stay away from Heidi? I've let my hair grow back for her so her family would accept me again. I've put off the change for her and dealt with all the times she's ignored what I'm saying only to talk about her own problems. And why won't she call me Troy?

I've given up a huge part of myself so we could be one.

JC's probably already there. I'm sure she called him.

All the bad thoughts make me sick and tired. I close my eyes as tight as possible and pray that sleep will make everything go away.

Before the sun is up, I open my eyes—I'm ready to go back. It's not even six. Dad's still sleeping, but I sneak down the stairs and scribble a note saying I've gone to Clauss field to practice. As I'm leaving, the coffee maker turns on automatically and the kitchen starts to smell like Starbucks.

Before he wakes up, I head outside and jump on my board, riding it down toward the middle of the street. The Sunday morning silence—no cars or door slams or loud giggles—gives me this eerie feeling like when I get to the forest I'm going to walk up on a JC and Heidi lovefest.

When I arrive, the park gates are still closed so I slip underneath the barricades and find the trail.

Fog blankets the low areas of the forest, and when I get off my board, it's like I'm walking through a light mist of feathery clouds. The ladder-looking tree that Heidi was reading in stands tall in the distance. But even from far away, it looks like she's not up there anymore. At least she probably climbed down to sleep. And then that painful feeling comes back to my heart again. What if I walk in on heartbreak?

From a distance the book light glows a dim circle near the ground. Something inside tells me to get there fast.

When I reach Heidi she's at the bottom of the tree, face planted in the ground. Blood stains her chin and lip. "Heidi!" I cry.

She mumbles something and tries to open her eyes.

"Heidi!" I turn her over so she's lying on her back. Her face is an iridescent shade of greenish grey. She mumbles again.

I lift her hair from her forehead. Dirt and blood are painted across her skin. The tree limbs extend high above us like a foggy-day crossing guard warning walkers to stand back. Heidi's blanket dangles from a tiny limb—holding on and draping down.

On the ground, her book is four feet away, face down, far from Heidi. The light is still in her hand, her fist clenched tight around it. I lift her in a panic.

"Heidi. I'm here. Did you fall?"

"Mmm-hmm." Her head and neck are limp in my hands as I hold her.

There's no time. I have to call for help. I dial 9-1-1 with one hand while still holding Heidi in my arms.

"Hello. This is an emergency. I'm at Forest Trails Park and my friend fell out of a tree. She's not really moving. But she's awake. Please come. Please help. Please. Quick." The operator tells me to stay on the phone.

A few minutes later, I hear an ambulance.

25.

Here's the thing about being in love with someone whose family hates you: it sucks. Big time. As if standing in the waiting room, pacing, worrying, fighting tears, hoping, praying, crying and remembering to breathe isn't hard enough, I've got Heidi's family giving me the worst evil-eye ever. Like I pushed her out of the tree. Like I tried to kill her or something.

Part of me wants to run away from this bullshit. Pretend that, yeah, maybe I don't love her, and maybe I can just forget about my feelings and go on being the person I've always wanted to be. But then I think of laughing with Heidi up in the tree, or running through the forest playing hide-the-Funky-Fresh. I touch the outside of my pocket and feel a little bump where Funky Fresh is chillin'. I know I can't leave. That little plastic monkey wouldn't let me leave even if I tried, cuz that little plastic monkey represents all the shit with JC and all the shit with me combined. Funky Fresh is a toy god—All-Knowing.

Hamid looks my way and says something to his family

and I can only understand the word "majnūn." Thanks. If they'd only give me a chance to tell the real story, then maybe they'd let us be friends again.

I turn my head away from him and pretend to find interest in the waiting room television, while a doctor walks out of Heidi's room wearing scrubs and a haunting bright orange skull cap. His face is sunken in from what looks like worry. He takes a seat next to Heidi's father and mother. I'm still the dumbass who's standing, watching all this go on, but trying not to get too close just in case her father wants to strangle me or something. Although being in a hospital makes me feel a little better. Even if her family wanted to jump my ass, I'd be able to get treatment right away. But still. I don't want to go there.

The doctor steps away and a nurse comes to sit with Heidi's family with papers for them to fill out. They're preoccupied with whatever's in front of them and won't notice what I'm about to do.

The door to Room 1615 is closed. I push it open, finding an empty bed and a long curtain, drawn for privacy. I sneak inside the room choked by the smell of sterilization—rubbing alcohol and Band-Aids.

It's quiet except for the soft murmur from some machines—inhales and exhales of robotic breathing. Before opening the curtain, I listen to see if anyone else is in the room with Heidi, but I'm safe.

Standing at the foot of her bed, I want to hug her, but don't want to hurt her smashed up face. Her nose is covered in blue and purple bruises. Her eyes swollen three times their normal size. A tube sticks out of her mouth that looks like it's helping her breathe.

I lose it. I'm staring at my best friend, bloody and bruised, and it's all because I couldn't come back in time. Maybe if I wasn't thinking all that crazy shit about her and JC I would have come quickly. Maybe if I trusted her and believed that she actually wanted to be with me and not him then she wouldn't be like this. If I was there during the night, she wouldn't have fallen out of the tree. She wouldn't be here all fucked up. She'd be fine. If I wasn't in her life she'd probably be living a normal one. Not one with a best friend who's so madly in love with her she'll do anything for her— even if it means doing the wrong thing. But maybe since everything is tearing us apart we just shouldn't fight it anymore.

Life shouldn't have to be this hard.

Taking her lifeless hand in mine, I lock our pinkies. She moves slightly but doesn't open her eyes. Or maybe she tries to but they're too swollen.

"I'm soooo sorry," I whisper. She doesn't move. But I'm still gonna tell her what happened. I know she can hear me so I explain the whole thing, hoping that maybe my explanation will wake her or something.

"I should've left anyway and just taken the chance that Dad would catch me." I leave out the part about me thinking she called JC and they were in the forest together. About how I convinced myself that they were making out. And why would she need me there with her?

She moves her head, shaking it. I perk up. "No. You

don't think I should have left my house and risked it. Really?"

She nods her head in agreement.

Then the door opens. My heart stops. Her parents would kill me. I take a deep breath and close my eyes, hoping that whatever's about to happen isn't real.

"I need to check your bandages, Hafsa," a nurse says from the other side of the curtain.

I open my eyes and let the air out that I had held inside my lungs in nervousness. Leaning near Heidi's face, smelling the sterile gauze, I say, "I'll come back soon." She lets out a grunt.

I think I've escaped without her family seeing me, but then as the elevator doors open Hamid gets off just as I'm about to get on.

"I told you to stay away from my sister," he says. His thick brows scrunch in. His dark eyes piercing at me. "Who are you anyway? What happened to you that you look like this?"

"I didn't do anything wrong. Really, I'm the one who saved her. If I hadn't come back, who knows what would've happened."

He steps aside so we're out of the way of the elevator entrance, standing next to a fire extinguisher. "What do you mean, come back?"

"She was there a few days. Trying to stay as long as she could. Would've lived in the woods, I'm sure, if this didn't happen."

"And wait, you weren't gonna tell us. Ever?"

"I was tryin' to figure it out. When to tell you. But then I found her after she fell. I could've tried to save her myself, but I knew she needed an ambulance. I also knew that calling for help meant that she'd have to go home. But you guys could take better care of her."

Hamid rubs his forehead and wipes his eyes. I can't see tears. "I don't know. This is too much. What's wrong with her that she thinks life's so bad at home that she's gotta run away."

I bite my lip. "Maybe you should ask her." I find my way to the elevator. Hamid stares at me as the doors are closing.

"Don't come back to visit her. We won't allow it." The elevator drops down, and so does my heart.

26.

Whoever said absence makes the heart grow fonder should win a Pulitzer Prize or something. After a week without knowing how Heidi's doing in the hospital, or if she's home, all I have are memories. The good ones. The bad memories are pushed somewhere in the back of my head. All I can think of are the good Heidi moments. Mostly, I think of lying with her. Under the blanket. In the sleeping bag. On my bed. Her eyes with that small circle of gold around the black center. I've tried everything to get her out of my head, but nothing works.

That's the problem with loneliness; it's the worst pain because there's no sign of when it might end. It's not like getting hurt in soccer when I know the pain will go away with aspirin or sleep. Nothing cures loneliness but time. I know I'm going to have to learn to live without Heidi.

I head to an extra Saturday afternoon transgender meeting, trying to weave in and out of traffic to make it there by two. My nerves have me on edge, worrying what catastrophe might get in my way: maybe an asteroid will smash into my car or an earthquake will split the road.

There's a group in the lobby area in front of the clinic, drinking paper cups of coffee. I'm a little late and they've already started talking.

There are eight people, most who look on-the-verge like me, but one who looks totally like a girl. But I can still see his bulge in his tight leggings.

Some short-haired lady stands up and shakes my hand. She introduces herself as Libby.

"Hey," I say, wave my hand, and take a seat. "I'm Troy."

They all say hi's and hey's back. Libby has everyone introduce themselves, and what's awesome is that they all give the name for the person they identify with. The guy in the leggings says he's Hope, and I think it's cool that he gave himself a name that means so much. We're two people away, but close enough where I can see his perfectly lined eyes. Short black bob. Most of the people are TG girls. There's another TG guy like me, but I feel bad for him already. He's kinda red-faced, like bad acne.

He waves. "Hey, Troy. Kevin." I'm thrown off by his super-tight shirt and big upper arms. God, he must spend a lot of time in the gym!

We talk for an hour, going around the circle, sharing stories about times that make us feel out of place or like a freak. And what sucks is that most of the people don't have cool parents. Most of the others have to change their clothes at fast food joints before they get to school or go out. Except for Hope. Her parents let her wear dresses at a young age.

She's already started the change. Kevin, too.

But there's so much pain hidden behind transformed bodies. A super-tall girl named Virginia raises her hand. Libby nods for Virginia to speak. "I'm sick of being called a faggot freak. People spray painted my driveway. I even saw a Facebook status that said 'Victor Detrick is a circus freak'." Virginia fights tears through her quivering face.

"Group hug," calls Libby.

We gather close to Virginia, arms connected, and hold her in our circle.

We're all saying goodbye when Kevin comes up to me. "Hey. Wanna go get coffee or something?" I'm focusing on his clear blue eyes.

"Yeah, um, sure," I say. "Isn't there a place around the corner, I think, that looks like a coffee shop?"

"Java Soul. Yeah. Good coffee and live music. Totally cool hangout." I wait for Kevin to invite the rest of the group, but he doesn't.

It's just us.

Java Soul is super-loud and I love it already. The place is packed. There's a girl and a guitar and a small can for tips. Maybe five dollars in change and a couple of singles linger at the bottom of the can, climbing up the side of the aluminum. The singer looks up from her guitar and smiles at us. Heart melt.

We grab our drinks and find some seats way in the back. I'm reading the words on the table covered in marker. Signatures, poems, and quotes. And you know how you always look for the one thing that means something to you?

Amidst a ton of scribbles and signatures, I find the words, "Live. Laugh. Love." If it were only that simple.

"This is cool," I say to Kevin, running my finger over the black writing.

"Yeah. For real, though."

"Hey. How old are you anyway?"

"Eighteen," Kevin says, "You?"

"Seventeen. Another month until I'm an adult."

Kevin adds, "Yeah. I couldn't wait. I mean, I get why they make us wait until we're adults. But I knew I wanted this waaaay before I was old enough."

I'm glad he's getting to what I want to talk about.

"So. About that. What have you done so far?" I take a sip of coffee, but stop myself. "I mean, you look great. Like this is you."

Kevin tells me this whole story from counseling up to testosterone shots. I want to be into what he's saying but part of me is jealous. Like he's so lucky to be able to do this. I have to wait another four years. It bothers me all of the sudden—I feel like a fake.

"Can I ask you something?"

"Yep. Sure. Anything, probably. Unless it's about the penis thing, which no, I don't have one. It costs as much as a house, dude, and it doesn't even work."

I try not to laugh, but it's too much. "Whoa. OK. Glad you put it out there and all." I swallow my coffee. "Wait. So, like, we can get a penis, but it won't work?"

"Right. They'll do it here for almost two-hundred thousand dollars. But you can go to Belgium and get one for half of that. But still, in my mind, I'm thinking: Do I want to be homeless or do I want a penis?"

Now we're both laughing. "Major suckage," I joke.

"You're not kiddin'. My doctor and this other doctor were talkin' about it, tellin' me how beautiful these penises are and all. Big, too, I guess. But I still can't bring myself to that kind of money."

"Especially if it doesn't work."

He laughs. "No one wants a limp biscuit. Even if it is the most beautiful biscuit in the world."

"True that," I say and then tell Kevin my story about the soccer scholarship and all. He stares at me like I've killed his dog. Like he doesn't care what I've got to say. At all.

There's this awkward silence between the two of us. Which really isn't silence because the gorgeous guitar girl sings to her guitar, her face covered by long strands of brown hair. I listen to the lyrics about feeling love inside your bones while I reconsider what I just told Kevin. Finally he says something.

"Wait. So you keep putting off the change for this girl, and I get that, but really, if she's moving across the world do you think it's going to work anyway?"

"Easy, killer," I say, "What's with you and the truth serum?"

"I just spent too many years living a lie and can't see why you have to. Frickin go play soccer on a guy's team—be the first!—and maybe once you're yourself you won't care as much about anything else. You won't be as desperate, you know?"

I'm silent. My blood is boiling and my heart is pumping out of my chest like I drank some ephedrine shake or something.

I take a sip of my coffee, trying to relax, embarrassed that I don't have all the answers like Kevin. "Where are you from anyway?"

"Canada."

"Oh. That explains a lot. You people are always happy. Aren't you?"

"No. We just don't give a shit."

"That's where I'm moving." I look out the window at the crowded parking lot. "That's it. I'm moving to Canada and going through the change and—"

"There's more here for TG guys. Better doctors and stuff."

"Fine. Whatever. But I'll go there eventually."

We get into this whole thing about maple syrup lollipops and how everything in Canada is about maple leaves and maple syrup and happy winters. They build igloos on snow days. It sounds cool as hell.

Three hours later and Kevin is my new best friend, especially when he brings up that story on the news about the TG basketball player. Lightning strikes.

27.

I can't get the nerve to call Coach Shoals, but I send him an e-mail, asking about their transgender athlete policy. His response is pretty vague but he refers me to a trainer who handles TG athletes.

On the phone with the IU trainer, she tells me there's a chance I could play for I-U's guy's team, but not Division I. She continues, "But I know Wisconsin State has a Division I guys' team. And I know they're good. You should try it."

I thank her and ask a few questions, but know I don't have a choice. I'm gonna need to wipe Dad's dreams of going to I-U and put myself first for once. And maybe it's because Heidi isn't in the picture anymore. Maybe now I can make decisions on my own not based on what she thinks or what Dad thinks or Mom.

Maybe it's finally time to just do things for me.

After another visit with Dr. Confey's office, I learn I'll spend another four months as a guy to see if I'm ready to go on to the next level. I've never been so sure about something in my whole life.

On my way out of the doctor's office, my cellphone rings. It's Heidi's home number. I rush to a doorway and head outside before opening the phone. "Tirzah, this is Mrs. Chaudhary." My heart races. "We'd like you to come over." I finish the conversation and agree to come over right away. But looking at my clothes I wonder if I should change. Will they accept me in long shorts and a guy's polo shirt with a baseball cap? Doubtful.

I head home after the doctor and clean up a little. Put on a new t-shirt, roll on extra deodorant, and cover my hair with a cabbie hat that I bought a few years ago. But then my stomach feels sick, like I'm heading into a tragedy. Like something horrible is going to happen.

I stare at myself in the mirror for a while, at the new gender-neutral shirt and not-so-guyish pants, and my covered hair, and my covering up who I really am. There's nothing that Heidi's parents could say to me that I'd want to hear right now. Why should I go?

My eyes are glazed and pulsing in the mirror, like I'm looking at the face of someone I've just met. I want to run from this person that Heidi has turned me into. This person that is nothing like the real me—only a recipe of what people want me to be: one cup good friend, two cups star athlete, a quarter cup teenage girl, two tablespoons child of a broken dream.

Kevin opens the door to his condo and invites me in. The smell of corn chips and old socks makes me want to gag, but when Kevin sits on the couch by a massive tropical fish tank, there's no way I'm passing up a game of Wii bowling.

28.

I'm totally convinced that the only thing that replaces loneliness is self-centeredness. And there's something entirely awesome about having control of all of my emotions. No one else can hurt me. No one is close enough to me to have any sort of impact, and the only opinion that matters is mine. I've grown imaginary balls living as a guy. So when I call Wisconsin State to put myself on the list for guy's soccer try-outs, it's like I've just won a gold medal—already. Everything I've ever wanted is finally coming together. Finally coming true.

On the phone with Wisconsin State, I tell the coach my name, Troy Maxon.

"Maxon, huh?" The coach asks. "Why does that sound familiar?"

I hesitate, but tell him that I was going to go to I-U. "I'm in the process of transitioning. I'm a transgender male," I say, sounding all confident and professor-like.

"Oh, right. Wow. Well, I know we've had an identifying female play on the girls' team, but never an identifying male.

But you know what? I say it's worth a try."

He tells me to show up in two weeks, and I ask one last thing. "Hey, coach." I say. "Do you think that maybe I could start over completely with my name and all? I know I've been all over the papers and I just don't want people judging me and all about my switch. You know, like the people that I played against and whatever on the girls' teams. I mean, they could try to take away our trophies and say that we had a guy playing on a girls' team. Couldn't they?"

"Oh, I don't know about that. I mean, technically you were a girl when you were on the girls' team, right?"

I agree with the coach and then say, "Right. But how about you put me down as Troy Mason so eventually we could say it was a typo or something, but right now I just don't want anything to jeopardize it, you know?"

"You got it, Mason," the coach answers. "See you soon."

I thank the coach and check the calendar: two weeks until walk-on try-outs.

Three days later, there's a blurb in the paper about a gender identifying male trying out for the team at Wisconsin State. The article says the teen's name remains anonymous, but that he'll be at try-outs. Blogs on the internet are buzzing about it also. I can't believe the coach leaked my story. I wonder if it was intentional—like for publicity.

Kevin is calling as I'm scanning the net for more stories. "Dude, you're all over the place, man. This is huge!"

"No shit," I say, "Had no idea so many people would write about it. Even that one sports writer Bill Konigsberg blogged about it."

Kevin laughs into the phone. "I saw that, you asshole. Dude, this is monumental. Like the Brett Favre penis picture story, only bigger."

"I wish," I joke. "Favre at least had something to take pictures of."

"Shut it," Kevin jokes. "Hey," he pauses, "I'm coming with you."

"No prob, brah. Totally, you should come."

It's weird how you figure out who your real friends are when you need them most because just as we're leaving for Wisconsin State, Skye sends a text saying she's coming with, too. And just for fun, she's borrowed her cousin's vintage limo.

29.

We pull up to Wisconsin State's soccer field with only a half-hour before tryouts start, which is better, I think, cuz I've had little time to see who I'm up against.

Skye parks in the back of a parking lot. "Wait right there," she says.

I stay in the dark velour backseat and roll down the tinted window. "Driver, I joke, where are you driver?" Kevin slides from the opposite side of the limo toward the door.

Skye opens my door. "Your destination, sir. Your final destination."

"You sound like C3P0," I joke. "Kinda look like him, too, all stiff and shit."

"Be nice to your driver," she leans in and rubs my nose with her nose. "Simmah down and be nice."

Up on a hill, the field is packed with guys of all sizes. I kick at the limo's white-walled tire. "There's no way I'm gonna be able to play against guys that big. I'm like the smallest one here," I whine as I throw the joined laces of my cleats over my shoulder.

Skye switches the ball in her arms from one side to another and wraps her arm around my side. "You haven't even given it a shot, crazy. Just stop. We didn't pimp it all the way up here for you to wuss out." She looks at Kevin as if to cue him to say something.

"No shit, dude. You're gonna make history here and there's no turning back. You think those people storming Normandy stood outside Normandy and said they probably couldn't storm it. Or something."

I laugh and my cleat bangs against my chest. "Remind me to tell you later never to major in history."

"No worries," Kev says, "I'm going into waste management."

"You make good money doing that," Skye skips ahead. "For real, yo."

"I'm not joking," Kev responds. "Nowadays they have that robotic arm that lifts the cans so you don't even need to get out of the truck and shit."

We're almost near the white line of the soccer field and I can feel the collective nervousness from the other players, which makes me feel worse. We head toward a sign that tells us to register, and wait in line behind a long-haired guy with calves the size of giant turkey legs. He combs his hair with his fingers pushing it forward so the tips touch his nose, and I feel bad that his hair means that much to him. Shouldn't he be stretching or something? Shouldn't I, for that matter?

Some gorgeous Asian girl asks me my name, and Skye starts to say, "Tir—" but stop the slip. "Troy Mason." I say my pseudo-last name like I'm trying to convince myself and her at the same time.

She runs her milky white finger trace down a long list of names that start with M. "Right," she says, her voice excited. "Right." She shakes her head and puts a check mark by my name.

"Please wear this," she hands me two pieces of paper with the number twelve and my last name at the top—kind of like jersey numbers. "Just tape it to your back and front."

Skye steps forward. "I'll do it, T." And she grabs the wide roll of tape from the woman as what looks like a reporter stares at me from her spot by the side of the table.

Like a grade school game of telephone, the hot Asian lady whispers something to another trainer who then whispers something to this other guy with a whistle around his neck. He heads over by me and I try not to stare at his chia pet chest hair.

"Mason, right?" The coach asks. I nod my head.

"Were you the one I talked to on the phone?" I ask, trying to sound upbeat and enthusiastic like someone with team spirit.

"Definitely, hey, lemme introduce you to our TG trainer, who'll go over a few things." He nods for the hot Asian lady to come over.

"Lisa this is Troy. Troy, Lisa. All niceties aside, have Troy sign the waiver, Lisa, and let's get him out on the field and see what he's got."

Lisa agrees and pulls a form from the clipboard. "So basically you just have to sign this saying you are taking testosterone but it's only part of your gender transformation and not for any other performance-enhancing purpose."

Kev pushes my side. "Told ya," he says, as if it was all his idea. But maybe I wouldn't have done it without him.

I nudge him back. "Shut it," and take the pen from Lisa, signing the bottom of the waiver.

"Yeah, no, I'm not beefing up or anything, so no worries. Just part of the process."

"Totally understand," she says. "Alright, now head out for stretches and the coach will guide you from there." Lisa shakes my hand. "Glad you're here, Troy."

"Me, too," I say, and am about to say more, like how this is a dream come true for me and I can't believe I'm really here and does she know what it took to get me here. But that reporter-type lady comes close to me.

"Troy Mason?" She asks.

"Yep, that's me," I respond, and read her credentials: Stacy Urban, ABC-8 News Team Producer. I'm staring at her crystal blue eyes and horn-rimmed glasses, trying to figure out if she's Mom's producer. I remember being at Buzz when Mom was texting a Stac about sweeps.

Stacy continues, "I can't guarantee anything because I haven't fully gone over the details with my anchor yet, but I was thinking your story would make the perfect sweeps piece for July." She rubs underneath her eye and then glances down at my shorts. "The coach said you were coming out today for try-outs, and we'll see how it goes and all, but I just think this'll be something people will want to know about. We've seen celebrity transgender stories but not many local everyday people. Who wouldn't want to hear about the first Division One transgender athlete to make it on a guys' soccer team." She wipes an invisible space in the air with her hands, like a cheesy magician.

"Who's this for again?" I ask.

"My anchor, Missy Maxon."

Something bubbles from my stomach to my heart, like a clot of blood fighting its way out from my insides.

"Missy Maxon you say?" I smirk. "Never heard of her." The clouds move quickly while the sun bursts through, shining down on the soccer field.

Stacy waves a camera man over while the coach blows the whistle. "Hustle up, everyone!" The coach says. "We're gonna get started."

Skye and Kev put their hands out to slap me sweaty fives, and I sprint out to the middle of the field.

A few guys nod at me, sizing me up, but they're nervous, too, and once the coach leads stretches, there's no time to worry if the guys know about me. There's no time for anything but soccer.

After about twenty minutes of playing, it's like I've grown a pair of balls as big as the one I'm blocking from entering my goalie box. Playing with guys is exactly what I needed. They're rough and I'm rough and they kick as hard as hell, but I block harder. Nothing gets by me except one ball that flew in the upper right corner because I was looking at the camera guy filming the try-outs, thinking how I was going to handle the mom sitch.

We are dismissed for the day, but Stacy and the camera

guy still follow us to our old limo.

"Sweet ride," Stacy says. "Hey, can we interview you in the back of the limo, maybe? Or what if we rode with you to wherever you're going next?"

"We're going to Ballzer King," Skye says, "For some victory burgers."

"Ballzer King?" Stacy asks. "Never heard of it. Is that only something here in Wisconsin?"

Kevin giggles to himself.

"What?" Stacy asks.

"Yeah, it's only here in Wisconsin," I say.

30.

At home, I'm packing for my move to Wisconsin State, staring at the newspaper clip of Heidi and me near the Bean. I don't even know the person in the picture—so happy but unhappy. So sure but unsure. It's hard not to miss some of the best moments with Heidi, but from the spot where I'm at right now, all of my past events seem like they had to occur for me to get where I am now. Each broken piece helped create my future.

Tossing my books in a box, I'm stopped by the black cover of *Pink Elephants*, a book of poems from one of the most troubled and talented poets that Kev took me to see, Rachel McKibbens. I think of the pain she went through—running away as a young child, watching her father drag her stepmother through the broken window of a cab, and not speaking to her mother for over eighteen years. Guilt sits inside my stomach like a bad burrito. Am I going to ruin Mom forever by surprising her on air, sitting for an interview with her when she has no idea the transgender athlete she's about to meet is her former daughter?

But I gave her a chance—many chances—to see me for who I am and understand me better; she chose not to. She chose to let me go. And if she didn't want to listen in her apartment, maybe she'll listen on the air—where she can't walk away or close the door.

At the TV studio, I watch a girl named Adele put some tan-colored makeup on my cheeks through a five-bulbed mirror. I look like one of those chiseled male models, skinny with a girl's nose and lips. On the television screen in the right corner above a trunk of rainbow colors and liquids, clips of me guarding the goal at Wisconsin State's try-outs dance across the screen. There's a banner at the bottom of the television that says, "First Transgender Male Division I Soccer Player," with the word "Exclusive" glowing in white letters. On another television screen, I can see Mom sitting in a chair, re-applying lip gloss. She puts the mirror down and stares at the camera. "When is this guy gonna get out here already?" And a camera man responds, "If you watched the show you'd see what we're airing at the moment, Missy. See the b-roll with your voice over?"

Mom squints at a small screen to her far right, but returns to her mirror stalking.

"Prep our guest for air-time in three," a director calls over the loud speaker.

Adele drops the makeup brush. "That's you, handsome. Gotta get moving. Three minutes until air time."

Adele guides me to the side of the room where Mom is sitting, and I stay put for a moment, watching Chet

Cazinsky introduce the story. "In an ABC-8 exclusive, Missy Maxon interviews Troy Mason the first gender-identifying male to ever play for a Division One soccer team."

Adele walks me to my chair while a stage hand slips a microphone up my shirt. I suck in my stomach and pray he can't feel the duct tape under my t-shirt. Mom drops the mirror from in front of her face while the stage director points his finger at Mom. "Go," he says.

Mom stares at me. Frozen.

"Go," the stage director says again.

I smile at Mom and mouth the words, "I told you."

Mom coughs violently, waving her hand in front of her, calling out, "Go to commercial! Go to commercial!"

On the television screen, Mom is hunched over, coughing, and the camera fades to black.

An air freshener commercial comes on. "Cover up any household problems with a simple squirt of Mist Away."

If only a room spray could erase this mess.

If only.

If I were in her skin, I would crawl and form myself into mass deformity so no one could recognize me. My mother starts to do just that—hide inside herself. She folds her chest into her lap and wraps her arms underneath her legs.

"Are you alright, Missy?" The stage director asks, tip-toeing up to Mom. "Are you OK?" He begs.

There's a hyperventilating sound coming from the area between Mom's knees and the spot where her head is resting, like a wild gazelle finally captured by a lion. I can't let my mom look so pathetic on air. I can't let her career crumble and everything that she ever worked for fall to the ground when the video of her panic attack goes viral.

"I'll say whatever you want me to say, Mom, just come on pull your head up," I plead.

The stage director looks baffled. He puts up his first finger and says "One minute to air."

"Just tell me what to say, Mom. I can say I don't know you, whatever you want. Just please."

Mom turns her head to look at me, and her cheek stays pressed against her knees.

"Sit up, come on!" I pull her shoulders off her knees and prop her up, smoothing her hair and rubbing the part of her cheek where her blush came off. Her silence is killing me.

"Thirty seconds."

Mom holds up the mirror in front of her face and reapplies some lip stuff.

"In 5.4.3.2.1." The stage director points at Mom. She clears her throat and smiles my way.

"So sorry about my coughing attack," she says, "I just didn't realize my very own son was going to be our guest tonight. Had no idea, really, about many things it seems. Let's start there, shall we? So Tirzah, when did you decide to officially become Troy?"

I lift my chest, breathe deep, and answer, "Since I met a Tupperware lady named Aunt Bev."

Acknowledgements

Monica Ali's *Brick Lane* drew attention to families I wanted to know more about. Ali's insight inspired me to study Bengali literature and scholarship. Heidi springs from Ali's ingenious storytelling. Heidi's personality emerged from my niece's friend, who after running away, was kidnapped by her brothers. Troy was born from my high school friend's struggles. One day the world will accept him for his true self.

I am forever grateful for my friends with the SCBWI who remind me why I write and teach me how to improve. Thank you to Mark McVeigh for believing in Troy's story. Bill Konigsberg shared his knowledge on writing about sports; thank you. The NCAA offered important insight on their rules regarding transgender athletes; thank you. The Graduate School at Northwestern University's Queertopia: thank you for asking me to moderate a panel and welcoming me into your circle. Thank you to Caitlyn Jenner for opening your heart and sharing your journey in order to enlighten the closed-minded. Thank you to Dr. Jeffery Einboden, my mentor at Northern Illinois University who taught me the Qur'an. My partner at MuseWrite, Michelle

Duster, keeps me motivated, inspired, and challenged. My college students are the reason I wake up each day ready to learn and share; thank you. I am a small limb amongst a body of supportive friends who have spent years filling my heart with love; thank you, my dear, dear friends. Thank you to my boys for their quiet nights of cuddling and goodnight prayers. And thank you to my extremely supportive parents for encouraging me to dream. I love you.

About the Author

Trina Sotira is an Assistant Professor of English at College of DuPage and advisor for the literary arts journal, *The Prairie Light Review*. She earned her M.A. in British and American literature from Northern Illinois University. She is also an alum of Columbia College Chicago's Journalism Department, where she received a B.A. in Broadcast Journalism/Television. Trina has produced television news in Chicago and Rockford, and more recently written novels for teens. With Michelle Duster, Trina co-edited and contributed to *Shifts: An Anthology of Women's Growth Through Change*, featuring 35 nationally recognized poets, essayists, and fiction writers. The anthology was a 2015 USA Best Book Award Finalist. Her flash fiction appears in *Emerge Literary Journal*. *In Her Skin* is her first novel. Trina lives in the suburbs of Chicago with her two adolescent boys, two geckos, one Lab, and a fish named Beef. www.trinasotira.com

CPSIA information can be obtained
at www.ICGtesting.com
Printed in the USA
LVOW13s1738180517
535011LV00011B/1174/P

9 780989 960922